THE THREE
"We Investigate Anything"

*

Jupiter Jones, Founder

*

Pete Crenshaw, Associate

*

Bob Andrews, Associate

The Three Investigators
Crimebusters
available in Armada

THE THREE INVESTIGATORS ™

10
Long Shot

Megan Stine and H. William Stine
based on characters created by Robert Arthur

Armada
An Imprint of HarperCollinsPublishers

First published in the U.S.A in 1990
by Random House, Inc.
First published in Great Britain in 1991 in Armada

Armada is an imprint of HarperCollins Children's Division,
part of HarperCollins Publishing Group,
77-85 Fulham Palace Road, Hammersmith, London W6 8JB

Printed and bound in Great Britain by
HarperCollins Manufacturing Ltd, Glasgow

1

It Pays to Win

THE NOISE SOUNDED LIKE THE OMINOUS LOW RUM-
blings of an earthquake. But it was feet, hundreds
of feet, stomping the floor under the bleacher seats in
rhythmic, near-perfect unison. And then the chanting
began, faster and faster.

"Dee-fense! Dee-fense! Dee-fense!"

Pete Crenshaw stood on the floor of the gymnasium
catching his breath and listening to the deafening
noise. Every basketball game was exciting, but this
one was different. The score was tied, the players were
tense, and Pete knew the coach was counting on him
to keep Santa Monica from scoring.

BUZZZZZ!

"Time out—Rocky Beach!" the public-address announcer called.

Pete and the other players huddled up around
Coach Tong, the Rocky Beach High School basketball
coach. Coach Tong looked each player in the eye—
especially Pete.

At 6'1", 190 pounds, Pete was small for basketball.

He knew Coach Tong had taken a chance in making Pete a starting guard. But Pete had talent, and now he was one of the best players on the team.

"Twenty seconds left in the game," the coach said. Quickly he diagrammed a play on a notebook-size chalkboard, then erased it with the elbow of his sweater. "Now, what are you going to do?"

"Win!" the five players shouted in one voice, clapping hands and walking back onto the court.

Just for a moment, before Santa Monica came back, Pete watched the Rocky Beach cheerleaders. They were jumping and yelling and pumping the crowd up. The prettiest of them looked straight at Pete, pushing her soft brown hair away from her face. Then she actually blew him a kiss.

Oh, brother, thought Pete. I don't believe she did that.

The girl was Kelly Madigan. She and Pete had been going together for months and Pete still could never predict what Kelly would say, think, or do next. Maybe, Pete thought, that's why he liked her so much.

"Someone's trying to get your attention," said Bill Konkey, the other guard on Pete's team.

"I saw the kiss," Pete said, embarrassed.

"Jupiter Jones blew you a kiss?" Bill asked.

"Jupe's here—at a basketball game?" Pete said in complete surprise.

Pete's eyes followed Bill's pointing finger into the bleachers until he spotted two familiar faces. They were Jupiter Jones and Bob Andrews. Pete, Jupe, and

Bob had been friends almost forever. Together they were The Three Investigators, Rocky Beach's famous detective trio.

Pete couldn't believe his eyes. Jupiter Jones was at a basketball game—and he was *holding a girl's hand!* Not just any girl, either. It was Amanda Blythe—girl with a capital G!

This was a major news story, because Jupiter Jones was a total brain about everything except two things— dieting and girls. He had no luck with either. But there he was, holding a girl's hand and smiling away. He secretly waved to Pete with his free hand.

On Jupe's other side in the bleachers was Bob Andrews, who got an A in Jupe's worst subject. Bob knew all about how to handle girls. When he got his contact lenses a few years ago, he seemed to get a new personality, too. Bob had become one of the most popular guys in school.

The buzzer sounded its alarm, snapping Pete back into the game.

"Twenty seconds remaining," said the PA announcer. "The score is tied 70 to 70. It's Rocky Beach's ball."

Bill Konkey passed it to Harold Dixon, a forward. Okay, hang on, Pete told himself. Only 15 seconds to go. Suddenly the crowd groaned as Terry Nolan, Santa Monica's star player, stole the ball.

Nolan took it straight for the basket. He was going to make the winning bucket—with only 10 seconds left in the game!

Pete leaped into the air just before Nolan went up for his jump shot. The timing was perfect. Pete slapped the ball as it left Nolan's hand.

Thumpa! The ball hit the floor one time and then— *thumpa-thumpa-thumpa*—Pete had it. The crowd was screaming. Pete took off for the other end of the court.

Five seconds! Pete knew Santa Monica players were coming up right behind him, but he flew into the air for a lay-up. The ball dropped through the net. Two points and then the buzzer sounded.

"It's 72 to 70!" shouted the PA announcer. "Rocky Beach wins!"

The band started playing and the cheerleaders came back onto the court, cheering and dancing as the players rushed toward the locker room.

"What a shot!" Bill Konkey said, slapping Pete on the back. Pete nodded and smiled, pulling a towel around the back of his dripping-wet neck. But he let his teammates pass him by. He was dead tired—too tired even to hustle for the cold, stinging shower that would cool him off.

"Pete," a voice called to him.

Pete turned and saw a man, a stranger, in the hallway outside the locker room. He was a man in his forties with a muscular build. He wore a purple Windbreaker that had an old-fashioned script S in white on the left side. Steady blue eyes looked out at Pete from under the brim of a purple sports cap.

"Pete, talk to you a minute," the man said.

He wasn't from California, Pete thought. The detective in him was running on automatic pilot. The man sounded like he was from Boston. Slowly Pete moved toward him.

"Ross Duggan," the man said, shaking Pete's hand. "I'm the basketball coach at Shoremont College. Ever hear of us?"

"Sure," Pete said. "You're about fifteen minutes from Rocky Beach. You beat UCLA last season."

"Right, that's us," said Coach Duggan. "Listen, somebody told me to come take a look at you, so I did. I'll tell you, I liked what I saw tonight, and I want to put an idea in your head. You apply to Shoremont and I'll see that you get a full scholarship—everything paid for. And you'll play on the team as a freshman. We're not the biggest school, but after four years of what I can teach you, Pete, I guarantee you've got a good chance to play in the NBA."

Pete took his towel and rubbed his sweaty reddish-brown hair. Was he hearing right? This guy just dropped out of nowhere and offered him a full scholarship to play college basketball? Pete didn't know what to say.

"Just think about it," Coach Duggan said, handing Pete a business card. "Right now you're good, Pete. I could make you great, and you could help me make my team great. I'll be talking to you soon."

The coach turned and walked away.

"A very confident man," said a voice behind Pete. "I'd say he's someone who's used to getting what he wants."

Pete knew that voice right away. He turned to see Jupiter Jones. Bob Andrews stood there beside him.

Jupe and Bob looked like before and after. Jupe, the shortest of The Three Investigators at 5'8¾", was wearing brand-new dark blue jeans—even though everyone at school was wearing faded stonewashed jeans. He also had on a too-small T-shirt that said I EAT—THEREFORE I AM. And he had the paunchy stomach to prove it. As usual, his straight black hair was mussed.

By contrast, Bob was sporting the trendy look: a red polo shirt, which looked great with his tanned skin and blond hair, plus stonewashed jeans and loafers without socks.

"Jupe," Pete said, looking around, "what happened to Amanda Blythe? I saw you with her in the bleachers and almost had a heart attack."

Jupiter cleared his throat. "I concluded that she wasn't my type," he said, scowling.

"Huh?" Pete asked. "Since when?"

"Amanda was just trying to make Carl Thames jealous," Bob explained. "And since Carl is the dumbest guy in school, she figured the best way to make him mad was to flirt with the smartest guy in school."

"Oh," Pete said, and laughed. "Did it work?"

"As a matter of fact, yes," Jupiter said, holding his stomach and wincing.

"You're lucky Carl just hit you in the gut," Bob said. "I thought he was going to rip your head off and go bowling with it."

Jupe sighed and changed the subject. "Who was that guy in the purple jacket?" he asked Pete.

"Coach Duggan, the basketball coach at Shoremont College."

"Did he come to say how totally awesome you were tonight? Because you were," Bob said, imitating a jump shot with an imaginary ball. "You won the game and made Terry Nolan look like a total geek all in one radical play."

Pete smiled as he remembered the final seconds of the game. "Yeah, I was pretty good, wasn't I? And are you guys ready for this? Coach Duggan just offered me a full scholarship to play at Shoremont College. He said I could play as a *freshman*."

"Wow!" Bob said. "That's incredible!"

Jupe pinched his lower lip in thought. "A full college scholarship just to play basketball?" he said. "To throw leap shots and make layouts?"

"To shoot jump shots and make lay-ups," Pete corrected his friend.

"Okay, so I don't know everything about sports," Jupe said. "But I do know one thing. If one school thinks you're that good, Pete, other schools will too. I'd advise against making a hasty decision."

"Other schools?" Pete repeated. "Jupe, I can't handle this. I'm going to take a shower and meet Kelly. See you guys tomorrow."

In the locker room all by himself, with the cold water beating on him, Pete replayed the game in his head. And he thought about what Jupe had said. Other teams interested in him? How many? Five? Ten? Wouldn't it be unbelievable if there was a bidding war for Pete Crenshaw, b-ball superstar?

When he was dry, cool, and dressed, Pete stepped out of the locker room.

"Pete!" shouted Kelly Madigan, running up and throwing her arms around his neck.

"Hey, babe," Pete said, giving his girlfriend a hug.

"Do you know how fabulous you were tonight, Pete? On a scale of one to ten, you were a twenty!"

Pete smiled. "Come on, Kelly. Let's drive. I've got something to tell you."

Pete wanted to get behind the wheel of his car because that's where he was always happiest—around automobiles. When he wasn't solving mysteries with Jupe and Bob, Pete bought old cars, fixed them up, and then usually sold them at a profit.

On the way to the parking lot, Pete told Kelly about the college coach who was waiting for him after the game. He was just finishing the story when they reached Pete's latest car, a twenty-year-old Cadillac Fleetwood. Pete had only had it a month, but Kelly had already nicknamed it the Ark. It was badly in need of repairs, which Pete couldn't afford to make. He had picked the car up as another one of his $700 if-you-can-make-it-start, you-can-drive-it-away specials.

Pete opened the door for Kelly—not just to be a gentleman but because he was the only person strong enough to open the passenger door. When he got in on the driver's side, Kelly handed him an envelope.

"Hey, what's this? It's not my birthday, babe," Pete said.

Kelly shook her head. "I found it on the seat."

Pete snapped on the overhead light and looked at the envelope. It hadn't been there before the game.

On the front it had PETE CRENSHAW typed in capital letters. Pete tore open one end of the envelope and shook the contents out.

"What?" Pete and Kelly gasped at the same time.

Hundred-dollar bills tumbled out of the envelope. A lot of them. As Kelly scooped up the money and counted it, Pete read the note that fell into his lap. It said:

"Shoremont needs you. Play basketball for Shoremont and you'll be rewarded beyond your dreams. This is only the beginning."

"Pete," Kelly said. Her face was confused and a little scared. "This is three thousand dollars!"

2

Fast Break

FOR A LONG TIME PETE AND KELLY SAT IN PETE'S OLD
Cadillac. They stared silently at the $3000, all
crisp new hundreds, fanned in Kelly's hands.

"What does it mean?" Kelly finally asked.

In answer, Pete started the car.

"Where are we going?" Kelly said.

"I've gotta tell Jupe and Bob," was Pete's answer.
He floored the accelerator, and after a pause the big
car lurched and chugged out of the parking lot. Pete
gunned it, heading for Titus Jones's salvage yard.

Jupiter Jones lived with his Uncle Titus and Aunt
Mathilda in a house across the street from their large
junkyard. At one side of the yard was an abandoned
trailer that years ago Jupe had taken over as The Three
Investigators' headquarters. Now that the Three Investigators were in high school, though, the guys usually
hung out in Jupe's electronics workshop, which ad-
joined the trailer. Bob called it Dr. Frankenstein's lab
because Jupe brought old electronic equipment back
to life in there.

Pete used a remote-control unit to open the big iron gates at the front of the junkyard. His old Cadillac rolled in and skidded to a stop. The engine died with a coughing fit.

Pete and Kelly opened the door to the workshop and found Bob sitting on a stool, listening to blaring music and reading *Billboard* magazine. Jupe was busy at his workbench.

"Hey! Listen!" Bob said when he saw Pete and Kelly. "This is the new band I might be managing!" Bob worked for Sax Sendler's Rock-Plus talent agency after school and on weekends. It often kept him too busy to work on mysteries when they came along. "What do you think?" Bob asked, nodding toward the speakers.

But before Pete could answer, Jupe snapped off the music. "They didn't come here to listen to music. Something's obviously the matter."

"How can you tell?" Kelly asked.

"Because Pete walked in holding your hand, which he doesn't do here in the office. And from the whiteness of his knuckles, I know he's gripping it very tightly."

"Jupe's recently become an expert on holding hands," Bob joked.

Pete smiled. He felt better already. Jupe always figured out everything. "Look at this, you guys," Pete said, throwing the envelope, the typewritten note, and the money on the table.

Bob and Jupe zeroed in on the cash.

"Wow!" Bob whistled as Jupe dropped the tiny screwdriver in his hands. Jupe picked up the note, holding it by the corner.

"Too bad you didn't check for fingerprints before you opened it," he said.

Kelly laughed. "Jupe, only you would check for fingerprints before opening your mail."

Jupe didn't laugh. Instead he held the note up to the light and examined the paper's watermark.

"Do you guys know what I could do with three thousand dollars?" Pete said, beginning to pace and talk. "I could practically restore my car to mint condition. I mean, the rear suspension is shot, I gotta grind the valves—"

"Pete," Kelly interrupted him with a push. "That money is a bribe. You can't take it."

"Hey, I know that, babe," Pete said. "But you can't shoot me for thinking about it."

"Man," Bob said, "you read about sports recruitment scandals at colleges, but you don't think it's going to happen here. Not in Rocky Beach, California."

"So what do you think, Jupe?" Pete asked. "It was probably Coach Duggan from Shoremont, huh? I mean, one minute the guy is saying 'come play for me,' and twenty minutes later I come out and my car looks like a cash machine."

Jupe put the note down. "Did Coach Duggan say anything to you about giving you money or leaving money for you? Did he look like he wanted to hand you any money?"

"Negative, negative, negative."

"Then logically we can't be sure that this bribe came from him," Jupe said with a shrug. "All he offered you was a scholarship, which is perfectly legal."

"So what's our next step? Call the NCAA?" Bob asked.

"No, I think we should report the bribe to the president of Shoremont College on Monday," Jupe said. "And then offer our investigative services to him. Cash payments to athletes aren't illegal—but they're unethical and completely against the NCAA rules. I'll bet the Shoremont College president will want to get to the bottom of this *fast*."

"Okay! Sounds like we've got a new case," said Pete.

"Yeah," Bob said. "There's just one thing."

"Don't tell us," Jupe said. "You can't come with us on Monday, right?"

"Right. Winter break starts, remember?" Bob said. "No school for two weeks. So Sax expects me to show up at the talent agency every day. But you know I'm with you guys."

"Only in spirit," Jupe said with a sigh.

•   •   •

Monday morning Pete drove Jupe to Shoremont College, two miles outside of Rocky Beach. It was a small, pretty, tree-lined campus. Pete was dressed for the occasion, wearing his red and yellow Rocky Beach High athletic jacket. Pete thought it proved that he really was a high school basketball player. Jupe wore a

Plato T-shirt with a picture of the famous philosopher on the front.

Pete parked the Ark outside the three-story modern red-brick administration building, and the two friends took an elevator up to the top floor.

"How may I help you?" asked the receptionist, a gray-haired woman with glasses stuck on top of her head.

"We'd like to see the president of the college," Jupe said. "It's a matter of extreme urgency." Jupe could sound very adult when he wanted to.

The receptionist buzzed the college president on his intercom, then led Jupe and Pete into an office with tall glass windows covering two entire walls. A man was sitting on the corner of a polished walnut executive's desk. He was in his thirties, young for a college president. He wore a shirt and tie, but instead of a suit jacket he had on a big comfortable cardigan sweater. "Hi," he said, smiling broadly as he walked over to shake hands. "I'm Chuck Harper. What can I do for you guys?"

Jupe simply reached into his wallet and handed President Harper a business card.

"The Three Investigators?" President Harper said. "I only see two. Well, what are you—a rock band? I do just about everything around here, but I don't hire the bands."

Jupe cleared his throat. "President Harper, I'm Jupiter Jones. This is Pete Crenshaw. Bob Andrews, our other associate, is unavailable. We're not rock musicians. We're detectives."

The college president looked puzzled until Jupe showed him the note and the money that had been left in Pete's car. Then Harper's face grew very solemn.

"I found it in my car right after Coach Duggan came up to me," Pete explained.

"Oh, boy." President Harper sighed and slumped down heavily on a large leather couch that faced one wall of windows. Looking out, he didn't say anything for a moment. "You know, I sit up here and watch my campus and think I know everything that's going on down there. But then something like this hits you right between the eyes." Then he was back on his feet. "Now listen, you guys can't just come up here and accuse my coach of bribing you. Prove it to me— prove it was Duggan."

"We can't," Jupe said firmly. "And we didn't say it was Coach Duggan. We're much better detectives than that."

"Well, it probably *is* Duggan," said President Harper, sitting down again.

The remark surprised even Jupiter. After another pause President Harper went on.

"The truth is—and this can't go out of this room— there was talk about Duggan using illegal tactics to keep talented players on his team at the last school where he coached. Nothing was ever proven, but that school's reputation was ruined. I knew I was taking a chance with Duggan, but I believed he was innocent. He's an excellent coach."

President Harper looked out the window again. "There he goes," he said, pointing to a figure in a purple jacket and purple sports cap. The man was walking one of the crisscrossed paths of the campus. "There goes Duggan."

Jupe and Pete went to the window and watched.

"Still," Harper went on, "he's got the money for a scheme like this. He demanded a large discretionary budget all to himself. He could be paying the guys and I wouldn't know. But I won't stand for payoffs at Shoremont!"

Down below, Duggan disappeared from view.

"Okay," the president said, "if The Three Investigators were going to investigate this bribe, how would you do it without being noticed?"

Jupiter didn't have to think about that one even for a second. "We'd cover the situation from the inside and the outside. By that I mean, on the outside Pete would open a savings account and deposit the bribe money. And he would act interested if and when he's contacted again."

"And what about the inside?" asked Harper.

"Simple." Jupe smiled excitedly before revealing his plan. "I'll enroll at Shoremont and attend classes with the basketball players. That way I can get to know them and find out who's taking money. It should work, because your winter term just started, and we're on a two-week winter break at Rocky Beach—so I won't miss any school. And I may even be able to tutor a few players."

President Harper shook his head. "Too hard, Jupiter. To pull that off, you'd really have to do all levels of college work."

Jupiter raised one eyebrow in reply.

"President Harper," said Pete. "There's only one thing bigger than Jupe's IQ—and that's the national debt."

President Harper smiled as he sat in the swivel recliner behind his desk. "It might work," he said, thinking out loud. "I could get you the basketball players' schedules so you could take the same courses."

Jupiter nodded and President Harper picked up the phone. He spoke in a low voice to someone in the admissions office. "I'm sending down a young man named Jupiter Jones," the president said. "Here's what I want you to give him."

A few minutes later it was all arranged.

"But *no* one can know about this," President Harper said as he hung up. "And I won't do *anything* unless you find absolute proof of Duggan's guilt."

"Of course," Jupiter said.

Just then President Harper's intercom buzzed. He picked up the telephone and listened to his receptionist. "Tell him I'll be with him in one minute, Ginny. Thanks."

President Harper hung up and rubbed his chin in thought. "John Hemingway Powers is outside," he said. "He's an alumnus of Shoremont, and he's just endowed us with enough money to build a new gym and sports complex. If he finds out about what you guys are doing, if he even thought there was a sports scandal brewing here, we wouldn't see a penny from him."

"It won't happen," said Pete.

"I just want you guys to understand the situation. This is top secret," said President Harper. He shook hands with them again. "If you need anything, call me. But don't come to my office anymore—it might blow your cover. And better use my private back door to get out."

Jupe and Pete slipped out the back door and down a stairway to the admissions office on the first floor.

"It's like a dream come true," Jupe said, beaming.

"It's a cool case, that's for sure," Pete said.

"Not the case," Jupe said. "College!"

3

Elementary Conclusions

WHEN JUPE REACHED THE ADMISSIONS OFFICE door, he turned to Pete and gave him a what-are-you-doing-here stare.

"We'd better split up," Jupe hissed.

"Split up?"

Jupe frowned. "Pete," he said, trying not to look at his friend, trying to act as if he just happened to be standing there, "I'm going undercover. I'm supposed to be a college student now. But you're a high school student. We can't let anyone see that we know each other. So will you beat it?"

"Yeah, sure, Mr. Megabrain. But you're not thinking ahead, Jupe. If I leave, how are you getting home? You don't have a car."

"I know that," Jupe said. "But I'm a college student. We're used to being independent and solving problems on our own. I'll meet you at headquarters tonight and fill you in—unless I have too much homework."

"You're the only guy I know who'd talk about homework and smile," Pete said, shaking his head. "See you later."

Jupe waited until Pete was out of sight before going into the admissions office. A few minutes later the admissions clerk had handed him everything he needed to become a Shoremont student. There was a student handbook; a totally confusing out-of-scale map of the campus; and a student I.D. card. But there was also something else—something that no other student at Shoremont had: a computer printout listing all the classes the basketball players were in.

Jupe went outside and quickly scanned the printout, circling the courses he would have to attend. Most of them were pretty easy—Introduction to Archery, Psychology of the Family Unit, History of Television. These guys take a light schedule, Jupe thought to himself. Where should I start?

The clock in the tower at the center of campus struck one o'clock. Jupe checked the schedule again. Walt Klinglesmith, a guard on the basketball team, had Chemistry 101 at one in the science building, Mars Hall. Now *that* was a course Jupe could sink his teeth into.

The campus began to fill with students hurrying on foot, on skateboards, and on bicycles from one building to another. Class change. Jupe had to hurry.

He stopped the first student who passed him to ask directions. "Where's Mars Hall?" Jupe asked. "I've got to get there fast."

"Mars Hall?" the guy said. "The science building?

All those nuts who want to build more bombs? Not my scene, man." And he walked quickly away.

College might be more of an adjustment than I thought, Jupe told himself. He took out his campus map and hoped he'd find the right place.

Mars Hall turned out to be an old stone building, nothing like the modern administration building. Jupe walked down dark hallways lit with an ancient lighting system until he came to room 377. It was a chemistry lab with rows of lab tables, each one equipped with sinks, Bunsen burners, chemicals, and glass test tubes. About forty students were sitting at the tables, talking and waiting for the professor to arrive.

Jupe walked in, half expecting someone to stand up and point him out: "Look! There's a high school student in here!" But no one stood up. No one shouted. No one even noticed him.

He slipped around the edge of the room, appearing to be looking for an empty lab stool. But really he was circulating, trying to figure out which student was Walt Klinglesmith.

He's a basketball player, Jupe thought. So he's got to be the tallest person in the class.

But that theory bit the dust. The tallest person in the class was a girl. She must have been 6'6". Her black leather boots were almost as tall as Jupe.

Okay, how about this? The basketball season is half over, Jupe thought. If it's been a rough one, Walt's probably got an injury or two.

So Jupe surveyed the room and *bingo!* There he

was. Jupe sat down next to a guy with a bandage on his wrist.

The guy had a leather-covered notebook on the table in front of him with W.K. embossed in gold in the corner. Walt Klinglesmith. Lying on top of the notebook was a super-expensive Mont Blanc pen.

Conclusion: Walt had money to spend. Where was it coming from? Coach Duggan's budget?

Just then the talking in the lab came to an abrupt end. The professor had arrived. A short white-haired man ambled to the chalkboard and began to write some words: DOG FOOD, LETTUCE, VINEGAR, SOAP . . .

Jupiter stared at the list. The items must all have a chemical compound in common, but he couldn't begin to guess what. College was going to be harder than he'd thought.

"Professor Wevans," a puzzled student began.

The professor laughed and turned to face the class. "No, this is not a quiz on elements. These are the groceries my wife wants me to buy on my way home tonight. I had to write them down before I forgot."

The class laughed, and the professor now wrote some chemical equations on the board. Then he began calling on students.

Stay cool, Jupe told himself. Keep quiet and keep a low profile. He knew the answer to the question, but he also knew better than to call attention to himself. If he didn't raise his hand, the chances were good that no one would notice him. . . .

"Wrong, Mr. Frankel. Absolutely wrong," Professor Wevans was saying. "Isn't there *anyone* who can tell me the answer to this equation?"

Jupe couldn't stand it anymore. He flung up his hand and called out the right answer.

"Thank you," said the professor. "That was the most exuberant answer I've heard in a long time." He stared silently at Jupe for a moment and then said, "Excuse me, young man, but are you in the right class? I don't remember seeing you here before."

Oh, no, Jupe thought, I've blown my cover.

"Uh, well," Jupe stammered, "I oversleep a lot and I've missed a few classes."

"Oversleep?" said the professor. "It's one in the afternoon. What is your name?"

"Jones. Jupiter Jones."

"Well, I certainly would remember that name, Mr. Jupiter Jones," said Professor Wevans. "May I suggest that in the very near future you buy a louder alarm clock?"

"I will," Jupe said.

"Mr. Klinglesmith, can you solve the next problem, please?" said the professor.

"Uh, sure," said Walt. He stared at the problem on the chalkboard. And Jupe watched Walt's face.

He's getting that look, Jupe thought. I've seen it a million times before. Slow panic, utter confusion, instant stupidity. He doesn't know the answer and this is my chance to make contact with him.

Without changing expression Jupe picked up Walt's expensive pen and casually wrote -2 on a scrap of paper.

Walt cleared his throat. "Uh, minus two," he said.

"Very good," said Professor Wevans before moving on to a new topic.

After class Jupe timed his exit so that he was walking out the door just a step ahead of Walt. In the hall Jupe pulled out the scrap of paper with the -2 answer on it and handed it to the basketball player.

"Want this?" Jupe asked. "As a souvenir."

Walt laughed. "Yeah, thanks," he said with a smile. "And thanks for helping me out. I could have figured out the answer, but my mind freezes when a professor calls my name."

Jupe's eyes twitched. Walt was handing him the Mont Blanc pen as they walked.

"Here, keep it," Walt said.

"Yes, but—" Jupe started to protest.

"I've got lots of them," Walt said with an almost embarrassed grin.

Interesting, Jupe thought, trying not to let his interest show.

"Listen, Walt," Jupe said casually. "Chemistry is all very logical. Maybe I could help you smooth out the basics."

"You mean, as a tutor?" Walt said. "Hey—that's a great idea. The only problem is, I haven't got much time. But maybe we could fit it in after basketball practice."

"I'll have to charge you, of course," Jupe said. "And a tutor of my qualifications isn't cheap."

"No problem, buddy. Whatever you want. Money's not an issue with me. Okay?"

Walt held out his hand to shake. On the third finger was a large silver ring with *Walt* inlaid in solid-gold script.

Jupiter shook Walt's hand, smiling as he thought, I don't want your money, Walt. I want to know where you get it. And you've got two weeks to tell me!

4

Kelly Calls a Play

THE TELEPHONE WAS ANSWERED ON THE FIRST RING.

"Three Investigators. You're talking to Pete Crenshaw."

"Pete," Jupiter said quietly.

"Jupe? Jupe, where are you? It's six o'clock. Kelly and I have been waiting at Headquarters for an hour. We're starving."

"I'm in the Shoremont campus bookstore. But the bus doesn't come for another hour. If I wait, it'll be two hours before I get home." Jupe tried not to sound too desperate.

"Oh, so you won't be here till eight," Pete said. "Okay. Thanks for calling."

"*Pete*, don't hang up!" Jupe said. "Listen, I need a ride, all right? Otherwise I'm going to be stuck here all night."

"But Jupe," Pete said. "You're a *college* student! I'm only in high school. You said we shouldn't be seen together. You said you'd solve your own problems and come up with a big solution on your own."

Jupe tapped his foot on the floor. "Well, that's the solution I came up with," he said. "You come and get me. Okay?"

"You know, you should get a car of your own, Jupe. You really should," Pete said.

That did it. That really made Jupe squirm. There was nothing he wanted more than a car—especially since his two previous cars had been totaled—and Pete knew it.

"Pete," Jupe said angrily, "if you don't come pick me up right now, I'll *never* tell you about the progress I've made on this case!"

"Is it good?"

"The bribes go deeper—much deeper—than we thought. That's all I'll say till you get here."

"I'm on my way," Pete said.

•   •   •

Less than an hour later Pete and Jupe arrived back at The Three Investigators' headquarters. Jupe was wearing a brand-new Shoremont College sweatshirt, which he had bought in the bookstore while waiting for Pete. On the way home, just to get back at Pete, Jupe had refused to talk about the case. A couple of minutes later, Kelly pulled up in her own car with two pizzas.

"Did Pete tell you exactly how I want my pizza now?" Jupe said.

"Yes, Jupe," said Kelly. "A mini-size pizza in a large pizza box. But what's the deal?"

"It's his new diet," Pete explained as he grabbed up a slice from the large pizza he and Kelly were sharing.

"Jupe, how many weirdo diets do you think you've tried?"

"I'd have to check my computer database, but I'd say twenty," said Jupe.

"Well, this is the weirdest," Pete said.

"It's the most logical," said Jupe. "It's called the Half-Weight Diet. You can have anything you want— but you can only eat half of it." Jupe took a slice of pizza, cut it in half, and put only one half on his plate. When he ate that half, he cut another slice in two and began to work on one of those half-slices.

"I'm having trouble watching this," Kelly said.

"Yeah, Jupe. It doesn't make sense," said Pete. "You've eaten two half-slices, right? Why don't you just eat one *whole* piece?"

"Psychology," Jupe said. "You wouldn't understand."

"Okay, Jupe," Pete said between bites, "so what happened at Shoremont today?"

"I've arranged to be the chemistry tutor for one of the Shoremont basketball players—Walt Klinglesmith," Jupe said. "It appears that he is rolling in money."

Pete and Kelly nodded.

"After chemistry, I sat through two feeble classes, trying to meet two other players. But apparently they both cut class. Then I went to the gym, hoping to observe one of their practices, but the team wasn't there. Only the cheerleaders."

"So what did they have to say?" asked Kelly.

"Not much," Jupe said, blushing and looking uncomfortable.

"He means he couldn't think of anything to say to them," said Pete. "So he left."

"Not true," Jupe said, looking down at his pizza. "I merely decided that the cheerleaders probably wouldn't know much and that I should focus on the team itself."

"Cheerleaders wouldn't know much?" Kelly jumped to her feet. "Earth to Jupe! Who knows more about a sports team than the cheerleaders? You think all we do is just jump around the gym and scream our lungs out? No way. We follow every play. We keep the crowd in the game. We cheer the team on. We flirt with the players. And some of us even date the players, especially when they're total hunks." Kelly grinned and gave Pete a hug around the neck.

Jupe wondered if Pete's face turned red from embarrassment or lack of circulation. "Well, since you know so much about cheerleaders, uh, perhaps you'd like to suggest a few conversational gambits I could use," Jupe said.

"You bet your pompoms I can," Kelly said. "First of all, you've got to charm them. You've got to compliment them. You know what a compliment is, don't you, Jupe?"

"Of course," Jupe said impatiently.

"Good," Kelly said. She sat down expectantly in her seat. "Well, go on."

Pete and Jupe just stared at her. "Go on and what?" Pete asked.

"Go on and compliment me, Jupe," Kelly said. "*Rehearse.*"

"Well, uh . . ." Jupe rubbed his hands on his jeans. "Well, okay. Uh, gee, Kelly, you're not as bossy as you used to be."

"He's hopeless!" Kelly sighed, rolling her eyes at Pete. "It's too bad I'm going on my ski trip tomorrow."

"Skiing?" Jupe interrupted. "How can you go skiing with a Rocky Beach basketball game coming up during vacation? You're the captain of the cheerleaders. Don't you *have* to be there?"

"That's what co-captains are for," Kelly said. "*You're* gonna need me more than my squad."

Jupe looked at her doubtfully. "Okay, Kelly, how does one, uh . . . charm . . . a cheerleader?"

"You have to win them over," explained Kelly. "Compliment their jumps, tell them their splits give you goosebumps—things like that. Then they'll tell you anything. Oh, and this is good, too. Tell them you felt as though they were looking only at you the whole time."

"Hey!" Pete said. "That's what you told *me*. You said you thought I was looking only at you every time I took a foul shot."

Kelly smiled slyly. "See. I told you it would work, Jupe."

The next morning Jupe attended classes, and in the afternoon he went to the Shoremont gym. He opened the door a crack, just enough to see that the basketball team wasn't there. But the cheerleaders were—five of them—in their short purple and white skirts.

Well, Jupe thought, maybe Kelly was right. Maybe he *could* learn a few things from them. He slipped into the gym and took a seat near the floor. The cheerleaders didn't notice him. They were in the middle of practicing a cheer.

> "Go, Cory! Go, Walt!
> You're the guys they'll never halt!
> Matt can shoot and so can Tim—
> And Marty's so fast we're sure to win!
> Go, Shoremont, go!"

I hope whoever wrote that isn't majoring in poetry, Jupe thought. Then he tried to get up the nerve to go over to the cheerleaders and talk to them. But he was sweating too much to do it. Anyway, the cheerleaders had stopped cheering and were talking to one another. All Jupe had to do was eavesdrop.

"Hey, give me a break," one of the girls was saying. Her long dark hair was tied in a ponytail. "You think I'm going out with Cory Brand just because he's got a condo and a Corvette?"

"Yes!" answered the other four cheerleaders.

"Well, can you think of a better reason?" the first girl said with a deep laugh.

Jupe's radar went on full alert. This was just what he wanted—they were talking about the basketball players! Cory Brand was one of them.

"Hey, what are you doing over there?" Suddenly a cheerleader with red hair and freckles was looking right at Jupe. She put her hands on her hips.

Jupe gulped. Okay, don't panic, he told himself. Stay cool and try to get as much information as possible. You've questioned people in dozens of cases before, and this shouldn't be so different. Just remember what Kelly said.

He got up and slowly walked over to the cheerleaders. As he came closer he saw that their names were embroidered on their purple and white sweaters.

"Uh, you know . . . Nora," Jupe said to the redhead. "When you were all doing that cheer, I felt like you were looking only at me the whole time."

"We were," she said. "There's nobody else here."

Oh, yeah, Jupe thought. How stupid!

"Well, what I meant was," Jupe stammered, "you have excellent eye contact. It's quasi-hypnotic."

"Whoa, guys—quasi-hypnotic. Hear that? When's the last time anyone called us quasi-hypnotic? Don't you just love it?" said a fast-talking girl whose sweater said CATHY.

"I know you," said a girl named Pat. "You're Jupiter Jones. You were in my Introduction to Shakespeare class today. You know what he did, you guys? He recited a whole Shakespearean poem!"

"Actually it was a sonnet," Jupe said.

"Whatever it was, it was *beautiful*," Pat said with a big smile.

"So what are you doing in here, anyway?" Nora asked. She was clearly the captain of the squad.

"Our practice sessions are closed," explained the ponytailed girl dating Cory. Her sweater said JERRI.

"Well," Jupe said, checking his watch. He couldn't tell them the truth—that he was working on a case! "I was meeting someone. But I guess he isn't coming. Sorry to interrupt."

"That's okay," said the smallest cheerleader—a tiny five-foot, blue-eyed, black-haired girl with a shy smile and a Southern accent. The name on her sweater said SARAH.

Jupe hurried away, wishing he could think of something more to say so he could stay and question them. He especially wished he could think of something to say to Sarah. She was exactly his type. But talking to girls was hopeless. It was *much* harder than prying information out of criminals!

"Okay, let's get back to it, you guys," Jupe heard one of them saying as he left. "And don't forget—look quasi-hypnotic."

A minute later Jupe was heading across campus to use the pay phone in the campus bookstore again. As he walked he made mental notes about what he'd just learned.

Jerri was dating Cory Brand for his money, condo, and Corvette. Did that mean Cory was on the payroll? Pat was in his Shakespeare class and would be easy to talk to again. Sarah . . . stunningly beautiful, small, dark hair, blue eyes, great smile . . .

Jupe was still writing the file on Sarah when he reached the phone. He put in a coin and dialed Bob at work.

"Bob, can you hear me?" Jupe said when Bob answered.

"Sax is listening to audition tapes—full volume," Bob yelled into the phone. "What's up with the case?"

Jupe could barely hear Bob over the heavy metal in the background.

"It looks like Duggan's handing out money left and right," Jupe said as loudly as he dared. "Some of the players have apartments and big cars."

"Really? Who told you that?"

"The cheerleaders," Jupe said.

"What?" Bob said, shouting over the blasting band in the background.

"I said," Jupe said, talking even louder, "most of the cheerleaders were surprisingly nice. And I think I have a chance to get a lot out of one of them. Her name's Pat. She remembered me from Shakespeare class."

"Jupe, I can't hear you at all," Bob said. "This is hopeless. Call me tonight." And he hung up.

Drat! Jupe thought.

Suddenly a pair of huge hands clamped down on Jupe's shoulders from behind.

"When I get done with you," snarled a deep, furious voice, "you're going to fit in a soup can—a 'chunky' soup can!"

5

Getting Physical

ALL OF JUPE'S SENSES WENT ON EMERGENCY ALERT. His heart pounded, his chest thumped. Suddenly the massive hands spun him around hard, practically lifting Jupe off the ground. Then the hands began to squeeze Jupe's neck.

Jupe wanted to fight back. But his instincts told him that if he struggled, he'd strangle, too. He craned his neck to look high enough to see the furious face of his attacker.

It was the big, gnarly face of Marty Lauffer, the center for the Shoremont basketball team. His greasy blond crew cut stood up in spiky sections that looked like miniature horns.

"There's been a mistake," Jupe gasped, hardly able to breathe.

"Yeah—your mistake," Marty said. He smiled for a second, showing crooked teeth with silver braces wrapped around them.

Marty was unbelievably strong. His grip was slowly choking Jupe, quickly turning his shoulders numb.

Jupe took a wild swing, pounding Marty once in the stomach. Marty didn't even flinch.

"I heard you on the phone. I heard everything you said!" Marty yelled, shaking Jupe back and forth.

I've blown it, Jupe thought as his face turned deep red from lack of oxygen. He's going to kill me because I've found out about the bribes.

Marty laughed and jerked Jupe around some more. "You're going to hurt for a year," he said as he cocked back one enormous fist, ready to swing.

Jupe couldn't help it. He closed his eyes and screamed.

"Marty, back off!" commanded a stern, angry voice.

The big hands immediately let go of Jupe's neck and gave him a push backward. Jupe slumped to catch his breath.

The voice had come from a man standing behind the basketball player. When Marty stepped aside, Jupe saw it was Coach Duggan. He moved in between Jupe and Marty.

"Young man, if you want to get aggressive on the court, I'll stand behind you a thousand percent. But if this is how you get tough with the world, then you disgrace yourself, and the team, and me."

Duggan spoke firmly and Jupe saw that his words had an instant effect. Marty looked down at the bookstore floor and stared at the tiles.

"Now what's this all about?" said the coach.

"I heard him on the phone," Marty growled, looking at Jupe with cold hate. "He was talking, uh, talking about my girlfriend."

Girlfriend? Jupe thought. *Pat* is his girlfriend? Was that the truth? Or was Marty trying to cover up about the basketball bribery?

Before Jupe could catch his breath enough to reply, Marty had mumbled an apology and fled. He disappeared through the crowd of students who were staring at the action by the pay phone.

Jupe and Coach Duggan looked at each other.

"He's got a temper problem," said the coach.

"You're telling me. You must have your hands full," said Jupe with a scratchy voice. He tucked his T-shirt back into his pants.

"He'll come around . . . with the right rewards," Coach Duggan said. "Important phone call? Talking to a girl?"

"Not exactly," said Jupe.

"Talking *about* a girl?"

Jupe nodded shyly to that.

"Call her," the coach said, almost as if it were an order.

Now? In front of you? Jupe thought. *No way!*

"I'm out of quarters," Jupe lied.

"Ah." Coach Duggan reached into his purple sweatpants pocket and pulled out a coin. "Call her," he said, putting a quarter in Jupe's hand. "Don't ever let something like money stand in the way of what you want."

Jupe watched Coach Duggan walk away. Generous with his money, wasn't he? How much of the phone call had *he* heard? Jupe had even mentioned Duggan by name.

Now Jupe was worried. He'd have to be more careful on campus, or he'd blow his cover before the case was anywhere near solved.

•   •   •

Jupe had a heavy schedule the next day, Wednesday. From eight A.M. to one P.M. he had decided to take five different phys. ed. classes. Each class had at least one basketball player whom Jupe wanted to observe. But it cost him. Weightlifting, bowling, gymnastics, track and field, wrestling—the workout was grueling.

And the worst part was that every class was wall-to-wall jocks—and every one of them was in top physical condition! Pecs, abs, bi's, and tri's all toned to perfection. Compared with the other guys, Jupe felt like a tackling dummy.

By the end of the fifth class Jupe had learned a lot. First, that he should never attempt more than two phys. ed. classes per day—even in pursuit of clues for a case. He also learned that not all the basketball players were rolling in money. Some of them seemed suspiciously rich, but others were obviously average. Jupe decided to focus on the players who were friendliest and easiest to talk to.

At two o'clock he dragged himself into a sixth phys. ed. class. It was a course called Colorful Speaking. The idea of a speech course for athletes intrigued Jupe, but more important, this class was a chance to question two more of the starting basketball players—Cory Brand and Matt Douglass. Based on conversations with other players that morning, these were two of Jupe's prime suspects.

Jupe arrived at the classroom and took a deep breath—to try and suck in his soft middle. Then he strode confidently into the room. He tried to melt into one of the seats in the back row.

The guy next to him was muscular, handsome, and sandy-haired. He was wearing some old jeans and a black T-shirt that fit tightly around his chest. The guy had round, dark tortoiseshell glasses. "How's it going?" he asked.

"Thousand percent," Jupe said, trying to sound like a jock.

"You new in this course?"

"Yeah. I'm transferring from another school," Jupe said with a private smile.

"Matt Douglass," the guy said. "What's your sport?"

"Jupiter Jones. Curling. It's a demonstration sport at Shoremont this year. You're in basketball?"

"And tennis," Matt said.

He seems like a friendly enough guy, Jupe thought. Let's see how he does under the hot lights. "I hear the guys on the basketball team here know how to party."

"We do our best," Matt said.

"Wild parties at your condo? Everyone says they're totally awesome."

"Not *my* condo. I rent a small room off campus.

Must be Cory you're talking about." Matt gestured toward Cory Brand—a tall, muscular, handsome guy a couple rows away.

Cory Brand seemed to collect things that began with C—condo, Corvette, cheerleader. Jupe was very interested, but he wasn't done with Matt Douglass.

"You going down to Tijuana for spring break? Someone told me that's where Shoremont students head," Jupe said.

"Spring break I'm holding down two jobs so I can make my spring tuition," said Matt.

Good, Jupe thought. At least he was asking the right questions. But Matt was giving him surprising answers. Jupe had now learned about four of the starting players on the basketball team. Walt Klinglesmith, Mr. Mont Blanc pen, obviously had money. Cory Brand, according to the cheerleaders and to teammates had money and was a party animal cum laude. Marty Lauffer was just an animal, period. Jupe hadn't had a chance to ask him about his bank account while Marty was strangling him. But now he was meeting Matt, who didn't seem to be getting any bribes. Some players had money, some didn't. What was the pattern?

Jupe began to sift his memory, trying to figure it out. Matt and Marty were seniors . . . Tim, the fifth starter, was a junior . . . Cory and Walt were sophomores. In his mind, Jupe ran through all the other players he'd met. It seemed like the youngest guys were getting bribes, the oldest weren't. The pattern didn't make much sense to Jupe, but it was a pattern worth investigating. Jupe glanced at Cory Brand. Yes, talking to him was a good idea—as soon as class was over.

A moment later the course instructor walked in and laid his attaché case on the desk. He was a handsome man with smooth, dark hair, and he was in great physical condition, too—probably a former athlete.

"Good afternoon, ladies and gentlemen, and welcome back to Colorful Speaking! I'm your instructor, Al Windsor!" He said everything in a loud, overly friendly voice.

Why was he talking so loud? Why was he trying to make everything sound so important and exciting? Suddenly it dawned on Jupe exactly what kind of speech course this was. It was a broadcasting course! All these guys were here to learn how to become *sportscasters* after their sports careers were over.

"The classroom conditions are perfect," announced Al Windsor. "And the players are at the pinnacle of their training. So I think we're going to have a great class for you today, filled with the kind of excitement you've come to expect every time you walk into this room!"

By the time the class was over, Jupe was exhausted from all that enthusiasm. He shook his head to clear it, then hurried out of the building to catch up with Cory Brand.

"Cory," Jupe called.

The tall, muscular guy turned around. His blond

hair was cut so short that the sun made his scalp
glisten.

"Someone told me that you're the guy to talk to
about joining a 'Vette club," Jupe said.

"No, I'm not going to be a veterinarian. I'm basketball all the way," answered Cory.

He started walking away and Jupe hurried after him.

"I meant a Cor-vette club," said Jupe.

"Hey, you've got a Corvette too?"

"Uh, '72, mint condition, zero to sixty in five seconds, and you really know you've got a road under
you," Jupe said, trying to remember everything Pete
had ever said about Corvettes.

"Yeah," said Cory. "And when you put the pedal to
the metal and kick in the afterburners, it's real loud!"

Jupe shuddered. How could someone with a 30¢
vocabulary of sports clichés have a $50,000 car?

"You got yours in the parking lot?" asked Cory.

"Uh, no. I left mine at home—in Alaska."

"You mean you're a foreign-exchange student or
something?" Cory said. "Come on. I'll show you my
pride and joy."

As they walked across campus to a student parking
area, Jupe tried to get information out of Cory, but it
was like trying to catch goldfish barehanded. Cory
talked and talked and never said anything worth hearing. Finally Jupe just came right out and asked him a
leading question.

"Cory, is Coach Duggan a generous guy? I mean,
did he ever give you anything?"

"Well, Coach gave me some free advice once. He said I should take this speech course," Cory said as he opened the door to his Corvette.

Jupe looked down and happened to notice Cory's Rolex watch. "Oh, brother, I'm really late. I told someone I'd meet them at three."

"I'll give you a ride in my 'Vette," Cory Brand said. "Hey—I just remembered. That's something else Coach gave me."

Jupe couldn't believe his ears. Had Cory Brand just admitted that Coach Duggan had given him the Corvette?

"Yeah, Coach Duggan gave me a ride once, when my 'Vetter was on the injured-reserved list," Cory said. He hopped into his red Corvette convertible in a single bound. "Jump in. Where are we going?"

"Nowhere fast," Jupe grumbled.

6

A Break in the Case

AT THREE FORTY-FIVE JUPE DASHED INTO THE
Shoremont gym looking for Bob. The two of
them were going to make an all-out effort today to
learn more about Duggan. Jupe hoped that when he
got there, he'd find Bob hard at work on the case—
maybe snooping around Coach Duggan's office or
grilling one of the players.

But when Jupe walked into the gym, he found Bob
doing what Bob did best these days—talking to girls.
He was sitting on the bleachers chatting up the cheerleaders. Of course.

"Hey, Jupe," Bob said.

"Hey, look, you guys! It's Jupiter Jones!" squealed
one of the cheerleaders. The others looked over at
Jupe and giggled.

"I'm late," Jupe said to Bob.

"I wasn't bored," Bob said. He smiled at the girls
around him, who smiled back.

"Let's talk," Jupe said.

The cheerleaders began practicing their cheers

while Jupe and Bob climbed to the top row of bleacher seats.

"I want to get into Duggan's office right away," Jupe said. "I don't suppose you've had a chance to check it out yet yourself."

"Not true," Bob said. "When I was looking for you, I took a wrong turn in the gym and walked right into Coach Duggan's office. Talked with his secretary—a gorgeous blond senior on a work-study program. Duggan's office is a busy place—lots of phone calls, people in and out—so I didn't learn much. But I did turn up one thing. Every week Duggan makes out a scouting report with the names of high school players he wants to recruit. He's got it all on a computer in his private office. I took a look at a report, and guess whose name was at the top?"

"Mine?" Jupe said sarcastically.

"Pete's. Duggan wants him to come to Shoremont in a big way," Bob said.

"Then why hasn't he made contact with Pete since last Friday?"

"I don't know," Bob said with a shrug.

"This is important, Bob: Did you see any notations or marks or codes indicating which players Duggan's giving money to?"

Bob shook his head.

"I'm beginning to have a theory," Jupe said. "There's a pattern here. The younger players are getting money and the older ones aren't. I think that's because Duggan is new at the school. He's only been here two years, I found out from one of the guys in my wrestling class. That means he hasn't been recruiting players very long. So only the younger guys—the newer recruits—are on his payroll."

"That's good," Bob said. "But it doesn't really *prove* that Duggan's our man, does it?"

"Not quite," Jupe said. "Circumstantial evidence. Not the conclusive proof President Harper is waiting for."

"Don't worry, Jupe. We'll get a break in this case. We always do."

"You can't wait for breaks. You have to make them happen," Jupe said. "Come on—I want to see Duggan's office for myself."

Jupe stood up to leave, but just then a figure came charging out from the locker room. He was dressed in an oversized green, purple, and white parrot costume. He looked so comical that Jupe automatically sat down again—almost as if he'd been knocked down by the parrot's ridiculous appearance.

"Who's *that*?" Jupe asked.

"Beats me," Bob said. "Looks like some kind of goofy mascot."

The parrot gave each of the cheerleaders a hug. Then he started running around the gym, doing cartwheels and jumps. But while the cheerleaders were forming a human pyramid, the mascot did a back flip and landed badly.

"Aarrrgh!" he screamed in pain, rolling and holding his leg. "My leg! It's my leg!"

"Uh-oh," Jupe said, jumping to his feet and running down the bleacher steps as fast as he could.

The cheerleaders quickly gathered around the parrot. By the time Jupe and Bob reached the floor, Nora had removed the parrot's costume head and was trying to help the guy stand up.

"I think I broke it," the guy moaned.

"It doesn't look broken," Jupe said with authority. "I'd say a badly sprained ankle."

"Let's get Steve over to the health center," said Cathy, talking a mile a minute. "This could be a real tough break, if you know what I mean." She and Pat helped the Shoremont parrot limp out of the gym.

"Poor Steve," Sarah said in her sweet Southern voice. But she was looking right at Jupe when she said it.

"Poor everybody," Nora said. "Now we don't have a mascot for the game. How are we going to find another parrot by tomorrow?"

"Whoa, guys," Bob said, stepping into the middle of the crowd. "Not to worry. I'm sure our friend here, Jupiter Jones, would be honored to be your mascot."

Jupe aimed his eyes like flamethrowers at Bob. "Are you out of your mind? No way!"

Bob ignored Jupe's angry stare. "Let me reason with him a minute," he told the cheerleaders. He pulled Jupe quickly away from the group.

Jupe muttered under his breath, "Have you gone certifiably insane? I do not do cartwheels. I do not jump. And I would rather go to graduation in my underwear than wear a stupid fuzzy purple and green parrot costume!"

"Will you lighten up about fifty notches!" Bob said. "Don't you want to solve this case?"

"What's that got to do with anything in the Western civilized world?" Jupe said, astounded.

"Jupe, I said we'd get a break. Well, it's only a sprain, but let's not get technical. This is the perfect disguise! The parrot practices with the cheerleaders and hangs around the basketball team. Tell me that's not the perfect undercover setup. How can you say no?"

Jupe didn't say no. All he said was "Absolute total humiliation."

•   •   •

Jupe and Bob rode back to Bob's house in absolute total silence. As soon as Bob stopped the car, Jupe got out and went straight to the kitchen. He was already digging through the Andrews' freezer when Bob caught up.

"Where are the microwave hot-fudge sundaes?" Jupe asked.

"Jupe, you told me to hide them from you."

"Well, now I'm telling you to unhide them from me," Jupe said. "Aha!" He reached into the farthest corner of the upright freezer and pulled out a package of ice cream sundaes. He practically threw two sundaes into the microwave.

"Jupe, what about your half-portion diet?"

"No problem. I'm only going to eat *one* of them,"

Jupe said with a maniacal smile. He set the timer on the oven and pushed start.

Bob reached for the phone and hit number two on auto-dial. "Pete, it's Bob. Get over here fast. It's a binge alert!"

In less time than it took the microwave to thaw the hot-fudge sundaes, Pete arrived.

"How'd you get here so fast?" Bob said as Pete charged through the door.

"Hey, the Ark has a V-8 engine," Pete said.

"Yeah," Bob said, "but it drives like it's running on V8 *juice*."

Pete laughed and spied the hot-fudge sundaes in the microwave. "Hey, thanks, guys," he said. He had one half-eaten by the time he reached the table and swung his leg over to sit down backward on a chair. "What's the crisis?"

Bob answered. "I volunteered Jupe to be the Shoremont mascot at the basketball game tomorrow night. He's got to wear a parrot costume."

"He said *honored*. He said I'd be *honored* to be their parrot," Jupe moaned.

"Jupe, I don't think this parrot bit is such a bad idea," Bob said. "I mean, look how we hung around Duggan's office after Steve's accident and got asked to leave. But if you're the parrot, you have a perfect excuse to hang around all the time. No one will question you. And that's when we'll strike!"

"Fine," Jupe said. "I see the investigative possibilities. But what am I going to do at the game? I don't do back flips, front flips, cartwheels, handstands, or splits. Have you guys got any constructive suggestions?"

"Sure, Jupe," Bob said with a straight face. "Why don't you just do what parrots always do?"

"What's that?"

"Stand around making nasty comments while you preen and molt!"

7

Polly Want a Cracked Head?

"**T**HIS IS *LET'S TALK SPORTS* FOR A THURSDAY NIGHT. IT'S 7:20 and I'm Al Windsor," said the radio announcer. "Back to our phones in a minute."

Instantly commercials started playing on Pete's car radio. Bob started singing along, and Jupe started grumbling from the back seat. "Al Windsor? That's the guy who's teaching my college speech class. Lose him! Let's listen to the news." He ruffled feathers on the Shoremont parrot costume next to him.

"Come on, Jupe, this is my favorite call-in show," Pete said. "And anyway, we'll be at the Shoremont gym in a minute."

"Okay," said Al Windsor, coming back on the air, "I've got Sam on the line from Hermosa Beach. How ya doin', Sam? Let's Talk Sports."

"Hi, Al. I'm doing fine," said the caller. "Listen, Al, I wanted to ask you about the Shoremont–Costa Verde basketball game tonight."

"Big game, a must-win situation for both teams," Al Windsor commented.

"Yeah, I know," the caller said. "But did you see the paper this morning? I mean, the Costa Verde coach—Bernie Mehl—was really laying into Shoremont's Coach Duggan."

"Yeah, I saw that," Al Windsor answered. "You're talking about the big headline where Bernie Mehl said, and I quote, 'Coach Duggan will do anything to win—and I mean *anything.*' "

"Right," the caller said. "Now, what's that supposed to mean?"

"Well, Sam, I can't crawl into Bernie Mehl's head," Al Windsor said. "But it doesn't take a genius to figure out he's bringing up those ugly rumors again—the ones about Coach Duggan paying his players a few years ago. It was a big scandal back in Boston, but nobody ever proved anything. And Duggan has been one terrific coach. My guess is, Bernie's just trying to stir up a little trouble. We'll see if he gets it tonight."

Pete slapped the dashboard with his right hand and the radio snapped off. "Hey, Jupe, this is getting intense. Do you think Bernie Mehl is right about Duggan? Maybe Mehl knows more than he's saying."

"I'm not sure," Jupe said. "But I did a little research on the Boston scandal today. From the newspaper accounts, it sounds like *someone* was paying the players. They just couldn't pin it on Duggan. Anyway, keep your eyes open tonight. Maybe we'll pick up a new clue."

"Okay," Pete said. "But I've been to Shoremont–

Costa Verde games before. They're always grudge matches to the death. You be careful, too."

"Pete's right," Bob said. "This may not be the best game for your parrot debut. Are you sure you want to go through with this?"

"Oh, fine time to be worried about my safety," Jupe said. "No, they want a parrot. And I'm prepared to give them one they'll never forget," he added mysteriously. "Just watch me."

Pete pulled into the three-story concrete garage behind Shoremont's gym. He wound around the ramps to the top level, and Jupe climbed out of the car.

"See you guys after the game," Jupe said. He wrapped his arms around the bulky bird costume and carried it over to the elevator.

A few minutes later, alone in a small room reserved for the parrot, Jupe began to dress. Outside in the gym, marching bands were playing and cheerleaders were stirring up the crowd.

"Shoremont!" half the crowd shouted.

"Costa Verde!" the other half shouted back.

Jupe listened to the crowd as he connected wires and put in fresh batteries and then attached a small microphone to his T-shirt neck. Then he put on the costume over his T-shirt and jeans.

"Testing one, two, three," Jupe said into the microphone. His voice came out of little speakers in his wings. It worked!

Finally Jupe slipped the parrot head on, fastening it with Velcro patches to the body of the costume. This was definitely one of the weirdest things he had ever done in his long history of crimebusting. But Jupe didn't care. He felt invulnerable in the costume as he left the locker room and walked onto the gymnasium floor.

A cheer went up the moment the Shoremont fans saw the parrot. Jupe could see them all watching him, waiting to see what kind of acrobatics he would do.

Sweat began to bead on his forehead. Could he really go through with his plan? He paused on the sidelines, not sure how to begin. Meanwhile both teams were warming up on the court.

Finally Jupe took a deep breath and ran out into the center of the gym floor. The crowd cheered.

"Uh-oh! Uh-oh!" Jupe called out in a harsh parrot's voice. "You lose! You lose!" He jumped around and pointed to the Costa Verde players, who stopped taking practice shots to see who was making that sound.

"Give up! Quit now!" Jupe the parrot cried in a shrill voice. "Quit now! You lose!"

The Shoremont crowd started laughing and cheering. A moment later they picked up Jupe's cry.

"*Quit now! You lose!*" The whole gymnasium seemed to be chanting.

The Costa Verde players looked stunned. One of them started to come after Jupe. But Jupe ducked and dodged, which made the crowd laugh even more. Then Bernie Mehl, the Costa Verde coach, came onto the court to tell his players to settle down and ignore the parrot.

But no one else wanted to ignore him. They loved him! Jupe jumped around some more, feeling bolder. Whatever the parrot said, the crowd echoed it. Jupe was leading more cheers than the cheerleaders!

When the game started, Jupe had to stay on the sidelines. But that didn't stop him from shouting his comments into the game.

"Uh-oh! Watch out! You lose, number 32! You couldn't even slam-dunk a donut!"

The crowd roared with laughter.

"Hey, number 52! Give up! Give up! Babies dribble better than you!"

Nora, the captain of the Shoremont cheerleaders, pulled Jupe aside.

"Be careful, Jupe," she said. "The Costa Verde players are giving you some mean looks."

"Who cares?" Jupe said. The show-off in him couldn't seem to stop. Every time a Costa Verde player missed a shot, Jupe would jump up and yell "Bird-brain! Uh-oh! Birdbrain!"

At the end of the game the score was Shoremont 64–Costa Verde 60, but Jupe felt like the real winner. All the cheerleaders rushed over to thank him. Sarah, with the short dark hair, gave him the biggest smile. Jupe was practically floating!

Jupe quickly changed out of his costume and hurried to meet Bob and Pete in the garage. He stepped off the elevator and saw them standing by someone else's car.

Pete's probably forgotten where he parked, Jupe laughed to himself.

"Hey, you guys," Jupe called. "Did you hear me tonight? I'd have to say that an appropriate description would be 'devastatingly funny.'"

"Yeah, we heard everything you said."

Jupe froze. That wasn't Pete and Bob. It was two Costa Verde players!

The two guys came at Jupe fast. There was nowhere to run—and no one around to hear him yell.

One guy grabbed Jupe, pinning his arms behind his back. The parrot costume fell to the concrete floor. The other guy grabbed Jupe's face and twisted his head around sideways. When Jupe cried out, the guy stuffed dirty sweat socks into Jupe's mouth.

The damp cotton smelled terrible and tasted worse. Jupe thought he was going to gag or throw up—and then choke on his own vomit.

"Now what do you have to say, Mr. Parrot?"

In the light of the garage Jupe saw that these guys were numbers 32 and 52—the Costa Verde basketball players he'd made fun of the most.

Jupe tried to scuffle with them, but they were too strong. They pushed and dragged him toward a low wall at the edge of the garage. "Let's hear you smart off now!" number 52 taunted Jupe. Then in one quick, terrifying move, they hoisted Jupe up and shoved him over the wall!

Suddenly Jupe was dangling in midair, held by his legs, looking down at the street three stories below. His arms flailed but nothing came out of his mouth except muffled screams.

8

Rolling in Money

"I LIKE THIS CASE, JUPE," PETE SAID THE NEXT MORNING, throwing his long legs up and across his kitchen table. He sliced most of a banana into his third bowl of breakfast cereal.

Jupe pushed away his half-eaten bowl of cereal and began eating half a sticky bun. "I don't find *anything* likable about this case," he said between bites. "For one thing, I'm sick of going to classes. It takes too much effort for too few results. Fortunately so many people cut class that no one notices whether I'm there or not.

"But what's even more irritating is that we're making no progress on the case. Last night I went over the note and the money we found in your car with everything but an electron microscope. Effort—one hundred percent. Results: zip. I didn't find one clue as to who sent it to you.

"Our next move is to investigate the typewriter in Duggan's office to see if the typeface matches the two notes you've gotten. But right now all we're sure of is that somebody knew you were at the game and knows what your car looks like."

Pete leaned farther back in his chair and wiped his mouth. "I can finish a whole bowl of cereal in the time it takes you to answer a question," he said, smiling.

Jupe frowned at the criticism. "Just what is it *you* like so much about this case?"

"I liked the look on the bank teller's face when I deposited the three thousand dollars last Monday. Today when I deposit a thousand more, she's really going to flip." Pete popped the unsliced remainder of the banana into his mouth.

"Well, don't get used to it," said Jupe, cutting a cheese danish in half. "You're going to have to give the money back."

"Jupe." Pete suddenly focused on all the half-eaten food spread out in front of his well-padded friend. "I really don't think your diet is going to work."

"It's working—slowly," Jupe insisted. "I've lost half a pound in the past two weeks."

"You probably *sweated* that off last night when those two jerks were roughing you up."

Jupe shuddered, and his stomach turned over. The picture of him dangling over the edge of the parking garage was still crystal clear in his mind. "If I hadn't been so overwhelmed, I would have fought harder myself. You and Bob arrived at the right—"

He was interrupted by the telephone.

"I got it!" Pete shouted to his mom in the other

room. He picked up the cordless phone in his kitchen. "Hello . . . Yeah, this is him."

"This is *he*," Jupe muttered under his breath.

"Yeah, I sure did," Pete said, snapping his fingers to get Jupe's attention. Pete's voice dropped. "I got the note and the money last night . . . Yeah?"

It was driving Jupe crazy hearing only half the conversation.

"Yeah, okay, sure," Pete said. "I'd like to meet you, too. Where and when?"

Pete listened some more, nodding, and Jupe held his breath.

"Yeah, I know where that is," Pete said. "In an hour?"

Jupe shook his head no and waved two fingers at Pete.

"How about two hours?" Pete asked. "Okay, I'll be there."

"Was it Duggan?" Jupe asked as soon as Pete had hung up.

"I don't know," Pete said. His face was angry and scared at the same time. "Sometimes it sounded like him and sometimes it didn't. He was real friendly, Jupe. The piece of scum is breaking every law that means anything in college sports and he acts like we're buddies."

"That's perfect," Jupe said. "It means he thinks you're playing along with him. Now tell me everything he said."

"He asked if I got his envelope last night, and he

said there was plenty more where that came from if I played ball with him. Some joke."

"Then what?"

"He said he thought it was time we meet and talk about my future, and then he set the place—ten minutes north of here on the Coast Highway. Why'd you want me to make it two hours?"

"Because the microphone I used in the parrot costume is a wireless mike. If I hook it up to a portable transmitter—"

"You can wire me for sound and hear everything that goes on!" Pete finished. "That's great."

"Let's get over to the workshop and hook you up," Jupe said.

Two hours later Pete turned off the Pacific Coast Highway at a scenic overlook. He talked the whole time he pulled into the parking lot, giving a full description for Jupe's benefit. Jupe was squeezed into the trunk of the big Cadillac with a radio receiver tuned to the same frequency Pete was broadcasting on. The trunk lid was tied to look like it wouldn't stay closed. In fact, it was tied that way so Jupe could get some air.

"Jupe, I hope you can hear me. Man, with this microphone and transmitter taped around my chest, I feel like I can't breathe. There are a couple of cars parked here. One's a Porsche 911 Targa. It's blue and it's bad. There are a few people looking around. One guy's standing by himself without a camera. I bet that's our guy. He's medium height. About thirty, maybe. Aviator shades. He's wearing a blue business shirt with a tie. He's got the sleeves rolled, and he's looking right at me now. I'll try to let him do most of the talking. I stopped the car. He's coming this way. Here I go."

Pete stepped out of the car, tossing his sunglasses on the seat behind him.

"Hi, Pete," said the man, slipping off his sunglasses and holding his hand out. Pete shook it, noticing the man had blue eyes.

"You want to talk in the car or look at the scenery?" the man asked.

"Uh, outside," Pete said,

"Fine," said the man, putting his sunglasses back on and walking back toward the railing overlooking the Pacific Ocean. "Let me say a couple of things. First, we think you've got the potential to become quite a basketball player."

"You've been talking to Coach Duggan?"

The man smiled. "Maybe the first thing I should have said was not to ask me any questions, Pete. I'm going to tell you everything I want you to know."

Why's this guy so calm? Pete wondered. I guess he's done this a hundred times.

"When we meet or when I phone you—and that won't be often, you'll know me as Michael Anthony." The man laughed. "It's a name I'm using just for fun, because Michael Anthony was a character on an old TV show. He worked for a very rich man who gave people checks for a million dollars. Anthony was the messenger, and he was never allowed to tell anyone who was sending the money."

"Uh-huh," Pete said.

"I'm working for someone, too, Pete, and I'm never going to tell you who, and you don't ask, right?"

"Uh-huh," Pete said again.

"Good." Michael Anthony took out a pack of gum. "I quit smoking," he said. "Want a stick?"

Pete shook his head no—then yes. Maybe he could get the guy's fingerprint. Probably Jupe wouldn't have thought of that.

No luck. Michael Anthony held out the pack for Pete to take his own stick.

"This someone is willing to pay you a lot of money to play basketball for Shoremont. You're the kind of player Shoremont really needs. We know you're interested because you've already accepted our first two payments. Well, to tell you the truth, four thousand dollars is chicken feed."

Pete gulped and almost swallowed his gum.

"But you'll never know how much your next payment will be. That's one of my employer's rules. But I'll tell you this: the better you play, the bigger the payoffs."

"And that's it? I just play basketball?" Pete said.

"The rules are simple." Anthony raised a finger for each one as he listed them. "You play like a star—that's first. You keep your grades up. We can't always help you in that department. But sometimes we'll tell you what courses to take. You never discuss our arrangements with a living soul—not your family, not your friends, not anyone else on the team. And you never try to find out who I am or who is sending you the money. What do you say?"

"Uh, I don't know," Pete said, following Jupe's instructions. Jupe had said to drag it out as long as possible. But Pete could tell Michael Anthony was getting impatient.

"Pete, you've had enough time to think about it," said Anthony, increasing the firmness in his still-calm voice. "Well, think about this: Every kid who plays college ball hopes he gets into the NBA. That's the only big money chance a basketball player has. And you know how many of the thousands and thousands of college players get into the NBA each year?"

"A hundred?" Pete guessed.

"Fifty. Not much of a chance to make the big bucks, is it? If you're smart, you'll make your college career pay off. And I've got a hunch you're smart, Pete. Now, I've got a basketball team to recruit. Are you on the team or not?"

"Yeah, I guess so," Pete said. "Can I let you know for sure in a few days?"

Michael Anthony chewed his gum for a minute. "It's a big step, an important decision." He put his arm around Pete's shoulder and turned Pete away from the ocean, until they were facing the cars in the parking lot again. "See the Porsche?"

"The Targa?"

"Yes. It's not brand new."

"I know. It's an '86, right?"

"Right. Pete, here are the keys."

Pete looked down. The sun flashed on silver keys lying in Michael Anthony's palm.

"What do you mean?" asked Pete, his heart shifting into a higher gear.

"The car's yours, as a loan right now. But it could be yours to keep, and I think you know what I need to hear for that to happen. Pete," said Michael Anthony, shaking Pete's hand again, "I'll call you tomorrow for your answer. Have fun."

"He's walking away, Jupe," Pete announced softly. "Slow. No hurry. Like he's got nothing in the world to worry about. He's getting into a new T-Bird. I can't see the license. I'm going over to the Porsche. No, I forgot. I'm coming to untie the trunk."

After Michael Anthony drove off, Pete rushed over to the Ark and let Jupe out of the trunk.

"I heard every word," Jupe said. He took some deep breaths of the ocean air.

"Jupe, come on," Pete said, rushing over to the blue sports car. "Come on. Do you believe this car? Do you have any idea what this is?"

"Of course. An expensive bribe."

"Okay, you can say that now, but wait till you ride in it!" Pete said, opening the driver's-side door and looking in. "Oh, Jupe. Oh, Jupe. Come on. Get in. Let's go for a ride!"

"Pete, are you nuts?" Jupe said. "He's getting away. We've got to follow him!"

"Follow him?" Pete asked. Jupe's words weren't making any sense.

"Michael Anthony," Jupe said. "We've got to find out where he's going."

"Oh, right, sure, no problem, great, okay, get in," Pete said. Now there really was a reason to drive this beautiful car. "No, wait!"

"Wait? But he's getting away!" Jupe said, running to the passenger side.

Pete ran back to the Ark and grabbed his sunglasses and driving gloves. "Okay, let's go," he said. He started the 247-horsepower engine with a roar.

"What about the Ark?" Jupe said.

"Let it rust!" Pete yelled.

9

Basket Case

PETE AND JUPE SAT IN THE IDLING PORSCHE AT THE scenic overlook.

"He's getting away!" Jupe cried. "Drive!"

"Hold on," Pete said, staring at the car's instrumentation. "I'm figuring out where everything is."

Jupe pointed in broad gestures and sounded like a kindergarten teacher. "This is the steering wheel. That's the gearshift, and down there is the gas pedal. I suggest you use them!"

Pete ignored him as he tried out every button and switch on the dashboard. "Jupe, do you know why lots of people wrap their new Porsches around a tree the first day they get it? They think driving this car is like driving any other car."

Jupe shook his head sadly. "Now I know why police departments never buy Porsches. If they did, they'd never go anywhere and never solve a case—exactly the predicament we're in."

Suddenly the car lurched forward with such force that Jupe felt welded to the leather seat. Tires spun,

spitting gravel at first and then digging in and launch-
ing the car like a rocket out onto the Pacific Coast
Highway.

"Wow!" Pete said, steering and shifting gears in
quick, precise movements. "I just barely stepped on
the accelerator."

The blue Porsche buzzed down the curving road
and kept accelerating as Pete wound out each gear.
Jupe watched the traffic ahead. One second a car was
in front of them. A blink later it was behind.

"I wanted you to catch up with Michael Anthony—
not beat him to wherever he's going!" Jupe said.

"What?" asked Pete. He was in another world.

"What color is his car?" Jupe asked.

"Oh. Black Thunderbird. Brand new," Pete said,
bringing the Porsche safely down to the speed limit.

Jupe leaned forward and checked the glove compart-
ment, the ashtray, and the map pocket on the door.
"There's no registration," he reported. "Not a scrap of
evidence that anyone owns this car or has even driven
it before. We'll have to run a check on the license plate.
Maybe that will tell us who Mr. Anthony really is—or
who he works for. Although something tells me that
name probably has been well camouflaged."

"There he is up ahead," Pete said.

"Stay far back," Jupe warned when he spotted the
black car. "We don't want him to know we're following him."

"Yeah, no prob," said Pete. "I just hope he drives
around forever. Is this car heaven or what?"

For a moment Jupe let himself sink into the firm padded seat and imagine the faces of all his Rocky Beach friends as he and Pete drove by. He could just see their looks of disbelief and envy.

"Hey—he's turning," Pete said, snapping Jupe back into the chase. "Right into Oceanside Country Club."

"Well, this is interesting," Jupe said. "The most exclusive country club in the area."

"Jupe," Pete said, braking at the start of the long, winding driveway that led to the country club, "what do we do now? They'll throw us out."

"Let him get ahead. Then we'll drive up and ask who was in the black Thunderbird, turn around, and leave," Jupe said confidently.

Pete pulled up to a valet parking stand in the shadow of an enormous white painted brick mansion, the clubhouse. Beyond the building lay acres of trees and grass with tennis courts, swimming pools, and an 18-hole golf course.

Pete stopped the car and lowered his window to ask one of the parking attendants about the black Thunderbird.

But the young man quickly opened the door for Pete. "Good afternoon, sir," he said.

Pete turned to Jupe with a look of surprise.

"Can you tell us," asked Jupe, "who was in the black Thunderbird that just pulled in?"

"Sorry," the guy said. "I just started working today. I don't know who anyone is."

"Well," Jupe said, suddenly sounding as if he

had belonged to the club for years, "he looked just like an old friend of my father's. We're going to go say hello."

"Sure," said the car attendant, handing a parking claim check to Pete. "Great car."

"Thanks," said Pete. "Want to see the engine?"

"Save it, Pete," said Jupe, leading the way up to the clubhouse.

Inside, Jupe and Pete stepped into a large lobby filled with comfortable chairs and couches, fragrant flowers, and soft music.

Slowly they wandered across the soft Oriental carpeting toward the dining room, trying to look as inconspicuous as possible. It was a huge glass-enclosed patio filled with round dark wooden tables and straight-backed wooden chairs with colorful seat cushions.

Jupe and Pete stopped in the doorway.

"See him?" asked Jupe.

"Yeah," Pete said, stepping back out of the line of sight. But he gave a quick nod in the direction of a small table near one window.

Michael Anthony was having lunch with a beautiful young woman. She wore a bright green dress that made her suntanned skin and reddish-brown hair stand out in the room even more.

"Maybe she's the one he's working for," Pete said.

But then Michael Anthony reached across the table to hold the woman's hand. "It doesn't look like a business partnership to me," Jupe said. "Still, I wonder if she has a direct connection to this case."

"Hey," Pete said, poking Jupe, "someone's coming this way, definite manager type."

"Probably the maître d'," Jupe corrected.

"I don't care if he's the welcome-wagon lady. He doesn't look happy to see us. What do we do?"

Jupe sighed. "I wish we could stay for lunch. The shrimp scampi looks delicious."

Pete and Jupe went back to wait in the Porsche for Michael Anthony. Jupe kept an eye on the steps to the clubhouse, while Pete set the radio presets and adjusted the graphic equalizer.

"Six speakers," he said, trying to impress Jupe.

"Five more than the House of Representatives," said Jupe, not very impressed. "Try to find where to put the key. Here comes our man."

Michael Anthony walked down from the clubhouse still holding hands with the young woman. But they got into separate cars.

"Follow her?" asked Pete.

"Follow him," said Jupe.

They drove south past Rocky Beach, past Santa Monica and El Porto Beach. Then Anthony got off the main roads and took several smaller ones that ended at a stone wall with an iron arch. The large brass plaque on the stone wall said COSTA VERDE COLLEGE.

Jupe's mind spun with ideas. It was as if after days of wandering around without water, he had suddenly come upon an ocean.

"Costa Verde—Shoremont's number-one rival!"

Jupe said, thinking out loud as Pete slowly followed the black car up ahead. "Here's an interesting possibility: Michael Anthony is working for Costa Verde College—maybe for Coach Bernie Mehl. Knowing that Duggan's reputation is already suspect, they're paying off Shoremont players to start a scandal."

"That's what Coach Duggan thinks. He practically said so in a TV interview after the game last night," Pete said.

"Really?" Jupe said. "I didn't see it. What did he say exactly?"

"He said something like 'Bernie Mehl's trying to start a scandal and ruin me.' "

"Hmmm." Jupe was silent for a moment. "Perhaps the bribery scheme is bigger than just one school. Michael Anthony may be the messenger at a number of schools."

Pete's face fell.

"These are just possibilities, Pete."

"Yeah, but if it's *that* big, we'll never be able to get enough proof," Pete said.

"Come on," Jupe said as Pete pulled into a parking place. "This is a start."

They had to follow Anthony on foot now. He seemed to know exactly where he was heading as he strode along the sidewalks of the small college. Pete and Jupe jogged behind, trying to keep him in sight and dodge the students walking by.

"Hey, you fat, featherbrained weasel!"

The voice was so angry that Jupe stopped in surprise to see what was going on. He saw four guys standing under a nearby tree. Instantly he recognized two of them.

"Uh-oh," said Pete. "Looks like numbers 32 and 52—the basketball players who roughed you up last night. No sweat. We can handle them again."

The four Costa Verde jocks dropped their books under the tree and started coming at Jupe.

"Hey, guys. I think Polly here wants a mouthful of broken teeth!"

"Pete," Jupe said, "I don't think we *can* handle four of them. My advice is run!" Jupe took off.

Pete followed, catching up with Jupe quickly. The four jocks were pounding the sidewalk behind them, gaining fast.

"They're going to pulverize me!" Jupe yelled, puffing as he ran.

"I'll split off and try to draw some of them away," Pete called.

Jupe ran as fast as he could, but he didn't know which way to turn to find the Porsche or the parking lot. So he just bolted toward a large lawn. Almost instantly he developed a pain in his side from running. He looked back and saw that only one of the basketball players had followed Pete. That left three enormous guys breathing down Jupe's neck.

Jupe reached a street and dashed in front of an oncoming car, then cut through an alley between two classroom buildings. But as he rounded the corner, hoping to duck out of sight, he ran smack into a group of Costa Verde students.

"Kenny! Grab that piece of dog meat!" a voice behind Jupe yelled. Jupe felt hands grabbing at him. It must have been Kenny, a guy in the crowd he had rammed into.

Jupe twisted away, but the collision had slowed him down enough so that now the three jocks were almost even with him. A moment later he felt hands grab him again. It was number 52, wearing a green Costa Verde T-shirt. He held on to Jupe and yanked him around. Then before Jupe knew what was happening, all three jocks were pushing him, punching him, and roughing him up.

Jupe struggled and squirmed, but it was no use. With three monstrous guys holding his arms and legs his judo kicks went nowhere. All of a sudden Jupe felt himself being lifted up and carried away. Where were they taking him? A moment later he found out. His attackers put him down hard, stuffing him into a wire trash basket at the corner of the street.

"That's where you belong, Polly!" number 52 said, kicking at Jupe inside the basket.

"Yeah—stay in your cage, parrot. And try not to mess up the newspaper in the bottom of it!"

All three guys laughed, then turned around and started to walk away.

Jupe was furious, humiliated, bruised, sore—and

sticky from something in the bottom of the trash basket. But before he could decide what to do, Pete pulled up in the Porsche.

"Hop in," Pete called, lowering the electric window nearest the curb. Slowly Jupe climbed out of the trash basket, got into the Porsche, and locked the door. He sat there silently for a moment, breathing heavily and dripping sweat. Then he noticed that Pete had a cut lip and a swollen eye.

"That fourth guy gave you trouble, I see."

Pete gave a small nod.

"Well, at least we got away," Jupe said.

"We're not the only ones," Pete answered, frowning. "When I got to the parking lot, the black Thunderbird was gone. Michael Anthony gave us the slip!"

10

Power Game

"MICHAEL ANTHONY SAID HE WOULD CALL YOU today. So we've got to be here for the phone call," Jupe said. He was busy hooking up a tape recorder to the cordless phone in Pete's kitchen.

"But Jupe, give me a break. It's Saturday morning," Pete said. "I can't wait here all day." He looked longingly out the window at the blue sports car in his driveway. "That car's not safe out there."

Jupe raised one eyebrow. "What?"

"Guys were calling me all last night begging to drive it—I didn't even know who half of them were." Pete was obviously getting agitated because he poured orange juice in his cereal instead of milk. "I told my parents the car's part of a case we're working on. You know what they said?"

"What?" asked Bob.

"They asked me if *they* could drive it!" Pete said, taking a mouthful of the cereal. "Everyone wants to drive that car."

"Yeah, I'll be happy to take it for a spin while you hang around here," Bob offered.

Pete rolled his eyes. "That car is probably the only reason you're here today and not working at the talent agency."

"That reminds me," Bob said. "Sax wants to drive it, too."

Pete was about to fling a spoonful of cereal at Bob when the phone rang.

"I told you he'd call," Jupe said. He jumped to turn on the tape recorder. "Keep him talking as long as you can, Pete. He's our only lead."

Pete switched on the speaker phone so they could all listen. But it was Kelly calling from Lake Tahoe.

"The skiing is great, but I miss you, Pete," she said. "Miss me?"

"Uh, sure," Pete said. "But give me a break, Kel. I've got you on the speaker phone."

"Oh. Hi, Bob. Hi, Jupe—I mean, Mr. Collegiate," she added with a giggle.

Jupe snarled at the speaker phone.

"What have you been doing? Working on the Ark, Petey?"

"Nope," Pete said, giving Jupe and Bob a wink. "As a matter of fact, I don't even know where it is. I'm driving something else."

"You traded cars already? That's a record. What'd you get this time?"

"A Porsche."

"Petey, we've got a bad connection. It sounded like you said Porsche."

"1986. 911 Targa. A totally cool blue."

"Come on, you guys. What's the joke?"

"It's true," Bob said. "Pete's got a Porsche. It's the next installment from the guy who's bribing him."

Kelly was silent for a moment. "Pete, if you care about me at all, you'll promise not to solve this case until I get home and drive that car."

"See what I mean?" moaned Pete, looking at his friends.

"The way things are going," said Jupe gloomily, "that's a promise he can almost guarantee."

At 10:15, the phone rang again. Bob answered. It was Valerie this time. She and Bob talked for about five minutes before they discovered that they didn't know each other. Valerie had dialed the wrong number. However, they still set up a date to go see a movie.

"When I get wrong numbers, they want to sell me magazines," said Jupe with a sigh.

A third phone call came at exactly 11:00. Jupe was nearest, so he answered. The voice on the other end surprised him. It was Chuck Harper, president of Shoremont College. The call-forwarding button on the HQ phone had bumped Harper's call over to Pete's house.

"Jupe, could you and your guys come to my office at four o'clock this afternoon?" Harper said.

"Of course," Jupe said. Afterward he looked at the

clock. Now they had the next five hours to wonder why President Harper sounded so worried—and why Michael Anthony hadn't called.

For the rest of the day the phone didn't ring. By two P.M., Pete was so fidgety he was driving Jupe and Bob crazy.

"Are you going to give up on this guy Michael Anthony, or what?" Pete asked as he repeatedly tossed the keys to the Porsche into the air and caught them again.

"I'm beginning to suspect he won't call," Jupe agreed. "He must have spotted us when we were tailing him yesterday."

"What a shame," Pete said, although a huge smile began spreading across his face. "All right, I'm out of here!"

"Drop me at Sax's," Bob said. "I can't make the four o'clock meeting. Gotta work tonight and tomorrow. And Monday."

"Right," Jupe and Pete groaned in unison.

The three of them piled into the Porsche and drove Bob to the talent agency. Then Pete and Jupe cruised until it was time to head for Shoremont.

The administration building was empty and quiet, as usual for a Saturday afternoon. Pete and Jupe found President Harper sitting behind his desk instead of on it. He was unbending paper clips at a rapid rate and wearing a very solemn face. With him was a second man, seated in a tall-backed leather chair.

"Jupiter Jones and Pete Crenshaw, this is John Hemingway Powers," said President Harper.

Oh, yes, Jupe remembered, you are Mr. Checkbook, who offered to pay for a new gym.

The man stood up. His height wasn't impressive. He had dark wavy hair and a small mustache. He looked like any successful business executive in an expensive blue suit—except for his eyes. They were dark and seemed to bore into the two teenagers as he shook hands.

"I have been informed by President Harper that you received bribery money to enroll at Shoremont," he said tersely to Pete. "And *you*," he said when his eyes turned to Jupe, "are posing as a student to find out who sent the money."

President Harper cleared his throat. "Mr. Powers and I played tennis this morning," he explained. "And during the match, he mentioned that he wanted to contribute an additional sum of money—to increase Coach Duggan's discretionary budget. I told him I didn't think that was a good idea right now and tried to leave it at that. However—"

Powers interrupted in a strong, to-the-point voice. "When someone tells me there's something I can't do, I start asking why."

President Harper continued, sounding slightly uncomfortable. "Well, finally I decided it was only fair to let John know about our suspicions. Fortunately, John understands and respects the way we're dealing with this problem. He has graciously offered to help with the investigation in any way he can. But of course he's as concerned as I am to avoid a scandal."

"Well?" Powers said, staring at Jupe and Pete. Jupe understood: John Hemingway Powers wanted to know what was going on—and he wanted to know now.

"I think we are getting very close to uncovering which players are receiving bribery money and who is behind the plot," Jupe said, putting on his most confident face. "A man calling himself Michael Anthony contacted Pete in person. He gave Pete a car—"

"A Porsche," interrupted Pete.

"And he also admitted that he is working for someone else. But we don't know for whom yet."

"Best guess," Powers demanded.

"Coach Duggan," said President Harper.

"True," said Jupe, "but it's also possible that Bernie Mehl is trying to frame Coach Duggan."

"Yeah. We followed Michael Anthony to Costa Verde's campus," added Pete.

"Guys, I don't care who it is," said President Harper. "I just want you to get the proof you need and settle this fast. We've got to clean house before this leaks out. Because if the press finds out, they won't *clean* our house. They'll *burn* it down."

Powers turned to President Harper. "Chuck, I'm convinced you're going about this the right way. I think these guys are on the right track."

Then Powers gave one of his penetrating stares. "I hope, young man, you won't get the wrong idea about

Shoremont. The things I learned here when I was a student helped me become what I am today. It's a wonderful school. And if you really are an outstanding athlete, we'd be pleased to have you enroll—but not for money."

As Jupe and Pete left the building Pete said, "That Powers is something else. I'll bet he could tell an earthquake what to do."

"I'm certain he'd try," agreed Jupe. "I think he expects us to solve this case by tomorrow."

"Tomorrow's Sunday. What are the chances?"

"It all depends on what I find out from Walt Klinglesmith. I'm supposed to tutor him in chemistry in an hour. See you later."

Jupe waited for Walt in the student center, going over strategies in his mind.

Strategy #1 was to pump Walt. He'd start with simple, casual questions. Questions like: "Who recruited you for the Shoremont team?" and "What made you decide to take the offer?" If a subtle approach didn't work, he might just come out and ask Walt about the bribes. Jupe figured if anyone was going to open up to him, it would be Walt.

Strategy #2 was a thorough search of Coach Duggan's office. Duggan was still the number-one suspect, but so far Jupe hadn't been able to get close enough to him to find out a thing.

Strategy #3 was on the back burner. It was Pete's idea—a full-fledged investigation of the Costa Verde coach, Bernie Mehl. Jupe had to admit it was a logical ploy. But as he told Pete, there was no way he was going to spend another second on the Costa Verde campus. Not with those Costa Verde jocks still hungry for the parrot's blood! Jupe suggested Pete investigate Bernie Mehl alone, to which Pete replied, "It's bad enough being the Two Investigators with Bob gone all the time. But the One Investigator? No way!"

"Hi, Jupiter," called a girl, bringing Jupe back to reality.

Jupe turned and saw Cathy, the cheerleader who talked so fast Jupe wondered if she were trying to break the sound barrier. She came up to him as he sat in the student center lobby.

"Hi. How's it going? You were great at the game. You're going to be the parrot again this week, aren't you? Because Steve's still limping around."

"Uh, gee, I guess so," Jupe stammered.

Cathy sat down close to him. "Jupiter, could I talk to you about a philosophy paper I'm supposed to write? I bet you have a lot of good ideas. What do you say?"

Just what I don't need, Jupe thought. Real homework and real papers to write! So far, by skipping around from class to class, he'd avoided doing any real classwork at all. And Jupe wanted to keep it that way.

Jupe stumbled around, trying to answer without saying anything. Finally Walt Klinglesmith arrived.

"Sorry I'm late, Jupe," Walt said. "Hi, Cathy."

"Hi, Walt," Cathy said.

"Jupiter, sorry, but I'm whipped. I can't study today. Coach practically killed us in practice. I'm going home to Z out."

Jupe frowned, hearing that his chance to find out more about the bribery scheme was going to take a nap.

"Hey, don't look so serious," Walt said. "Why don't you come party with us at Cory Brand's condo on Tuesday night? Big crowd. Bring a friend if you want."

"Good idea, Jupe. Maybe we can talk philosophy there," Cathy teased.

"Yeah, sure," said Jupe with a smile.

•   •   •

A party at Cory's condo—it sounded like a terrific place to get information about the case. But the case couldn't wait until Tuesday night. Time was running out and the pressure was on—especially now that moneyman Powers was breathing down their necks. Jupe decided to spend Sunday morning focusing on their prime suspect: Duggan. A trip to Duggan's office was long overdue, and the gym should be empty at that hour, Jupe thought as he hurried across campus.

Wrong. The sound of bouncing basketballs echoed through the halls the minute Jupe entered the building. Jupe peeked into the gym and saw the whole team. Duggan worked them hard, Jupe realized, calling practices all weekend long. No wonder the team was planning a party on Tuesday night. With a Sunday-morning practice they didn't dare party on Saturday night!

Jupe sneaked toward Duggan's office, taking the

hallway that ran behind the gym so he wouldn't be noticed. Maybe this was a lucky break in disguise.

Jupe's heart pounded. If Duggan came back while Jupe was snooping around . . . if Jupe got caught . . . it would blow the case and destroy his cover.

He paused in the hallway outside Duggan's office, looked both ways, then tried the doorknob. It opened. Quickly Jupe slipped inside and stood in the outer office. Now he had to work fast.

With slightly sweaty hands, Jupe put a piece of paper in the secretary's typewriter and typed a few words. Then he held it up to the light with one of the bribery notes behind it. Did the typefaces match? It took a moment to decide—but no. So Jupe moved quietly into the coach's private office and closed the door.

Immediately he powered up the coach's computer so that he could print something out and compare it with Pete's note. But the noise of the printer made him nervous. Could it be heard outside the office? Maybe. Worse yet, it prevented him from hearing anyone who might be coming in.

While the printer hammered away, Jupe went through the papers on Duggan's desk, being careful not to move them. He read memos, scouting reports, game-play books, and equipment invoices. He even looked through the coach's own personal checkbook register, which was sitting there in full view.

But three quarters of an hour later Jupe had to give up. There was absolutely nothing on the desk to incriminate Duggan. And the computer printout didn't match the note.

Now what? Jupe wondered. Did this mean Duggan was clean? Or was Duggan simply too smart for them? Or was there another suspect entirely—someone they had overlooked?

There was one other possibility, Jupe decided as he rode home on the bus. Maybe the mysterious Michael Anthony wasn't working for anyone. Maybe he was working for himself!

11

A Total Blast

ON MONDAY THE CASE CAME TO A GRINDING HALT.
It was a holiday, so there were no classes at
Shoremont, or at Costa Verde, either. Halfheartedly
Jupe called Coach Bernie Mehl at home, thinking
that maybe he could ask a few questions. But Mehl
wasn't there.

So Jupe and Pete spent the day hanging out at
Headquarters, playing video games and tinkering with
electronic equipment. It was the closest thing to a
vacation day they'd had since the two-week winter
break began.

Tuesday, however, was different. Jupe had a gut
feeling that something big was going to break in the
case. Maybe it would be a clue or a lead at Cory
Brand's party that night. Jupe spent the afternoon in
his workshop getting ready for the party.

When Jupe heard the workshop door open behind
him, he snapped off the VCR.

"Jupe, I've got news," Pete said, rushing in. "Hey,
what were you watching? An old movie?"

"No, nothing," Jupe said. He tried to change the subject quickly. "What's your news?"

Pete stared at Jupe's guilty face. "What were you watching?"

"*Nothing*," Jupe said even more firmly.

"Then why's the monitor on, and why do you have the remote in your hand? I'm one of the Three *Investigators*, remember?"

Jupe cleared his throat. "Okay, I *was* watching something."

"Let's see it."

Jupe tried to block Pete as he made a move for the VCR. But Pete dodged and hit the play button.

The video started and onto the screen came Jupiter Jones, standing in the workshop wearing blue jeans and a yellow T-shirt that said: I WANT A SECOND OPINION. Jupe turned around, modeling his outfit for the camera. Side view . . . back view . . . Then the picture flickered, and in the next shot Jupe was wearing a pair of bright-colored shorts and a T-shirt that said: IF LIFE'S A FEAST, WHY AM I ON A DIET? Then the picture changed again. This time Jupe was wearing sweatpants with a T-shirt that said: VERBAL JOGGER: I RUN OFF AT THE MOUTH.

"What *is* this—*The Jupiter Jones Show*?" Pete asked.

"Uh, no. Uh, our surveillance camera needed some repairs, so I was working on it," Jupe said.

"No, you weren't. You were trying on stuff to wear to Cory Brand's party tonight," Pete said.

"Absurd," said Jupe, turning off the VCR.

"Hey, they all look perfecto to me," Pete said. "But maybe we aren't going to the party."

"And why not?" asked Jupiter.

"I told you I had news, Jupe. Good news," said Pete. "I finally talked to our contact at the police station. Their computers were down all weekend—just got fixed today. So he helped me track down the Porsche's registration."

"Who owns it?"

"Barry Norman, 45 Lyle Street, Manhattan Beach, California," Pete said, handing Jupe a computer print-out from his back pocket.

Jupe double-checked the printout before saying, "Let's go talk to him."

The two friends climbed into the Porsche, and about an hour later Pete pulled up in front of 45 Lyle Street. It was a small four-story concrete and glass office building.

"You'd better park a few blocks away," Jupe said. "We don't want Mr. Barry Norman to see the Porsche and run. I'll wait for you in the lobby."

A minute later Pete pushed through the front door of the lobby and found Jupe reading the black building directory on the wall. It listed all the tenants in small white letters.

"Barry Norman . . . suite 421. This is almost too easy," Jupe said, leading the way to the elevator.

Suite 421 was locked. There was a gold nameplate in the center of the black wooden door.

"Barry Norman, Esquire," Jupe read. "He's a lawyer."

"He's going to need a good one when we're through with him," said Pete, knocking on the door. He knocked quietly the first time, louder the second time. And the third time he practically shook the door off its hinges. "Nobody home."

"I concluded that after the second try," Jupe said, already halfway back to the elevator.

Outside they climbed into the Porsche, but they couldn't see Barry Norman's building from there. So Pete cruised around to Lyle Street again and slipped into a spot near a pay phone.

Then they waited and watched.

Every time a man entered the building, they gave him a few minutes to get upstairs. Then Pete ran to the pay phone and called Barry Norman's office. No one ever answered the phone.

"Seven o'clock, Jupe. I've had all the sitting around I can take," Pete finally said. "He's not coming back."

"The logical explanation is that he didn't come back because he was in court or meeting with a client," Jupe said. "But I've got a strange feeling that something else is going on. I wish I knew what it was. But I don't think we're going to find out anything more today."

"All right! Time to party!" Pete said, revving up the Porsche. "On to Cory Brand's condo!"

"Not yet. I have to go home and change."

The party was going full blast when Pete and Jupe finally arrived. Jupe was wearing a purple and white Shoremont College sweatshirt—the one he had bought at the bookstore last week. Music was shaking the walls of the large modern apartment. And college students were talking and dancing everywhere—in the living room, in the kitchen, on the couches. Jupe spotted some basketball players and cheerleaders.

"What a great place," Pete said, looking around. "I'd love to have a college apartment like this."

"You could if you went to Shoremont," Jupe said pointedly. "Keep your ears open. This is an excellent opportunity to find out which players are taking bribes. And don't forget your cover story: you knew me *last* year at Rocky Beach . . . we ran into each other, and I invited you along. Got it?"

"Sure."

"Yo, Jupiter!" Cory Brand called. He pushed his way through the crowd to meet them at the door. "Hey, Polly want a cracker? Get it? Huh? That's a joke, isn't it?"

"You could have fooled me," Jupe mumbled to Pete. "Cory, this is my friend Pete."

"*Hi, Pete.*" Cory had to shout to be heard. "Hey, guys. Don't stand there empty-handed. Grab yourselves something to drink and let's party before the cops close us down."

Cory laughed and walked away. So Jupe and Pete wandered through the crowd. Occasionally Pete stopped to munch some chips and jalapeño dip, but Jupe kept circulating.

"Hi, Jupiter."

Jupe recognized the sweet Southern voice instantly. He turned around, trying to think of something clever to say. "Uh, hi, Sarah," he said. Someone danced into him, pushing him closer to the pretty cheer-leader.

Neither of them said anything for a moment.

"So how do you like your classes?" Sarah asked. She looked away from him. "Wow, that's a pretty dumb question."

"I've heard dumber questions, lots of them," Jupe said, with a smile.

"I'm . . . I mean . . . I'm a better listener than talker."

"Uh, me too," Jupe said quickly.

Sarah laughed. "Oh, you don't like to listen. I heard you at the basketball game. You were so funny as the parrot."

"Uh," Jupe said. How could the guy with the largest vocabulary in the school forget every word he knew except "uh"?

Suddenly Jupe felt a large hand grabbing onto his shoulder and shaking him gently back and forth. He saw that Sarah also had a hand on her shoulder.

"How's it going, guys?" said a dude with curly black hair that came down over his collar. He had a Texas accent and he was shouting in Jupe's ear. He reeked of beer.

Oh, great, Jupe thought. Just what I need—some big hunk coming over to put the moves on Sarah. How can I compete with him?

"Tim," Sarah said, "you've had too much to drink."

"Hey," the guy said. "I paid for all the food and beer at this party. And there's no law that says I can't drink it all! Who's your boyfriend?"

Sarah blushed and so did Jupe.

"Tim Frisch, this is Jupiter Jones."

"Howdy. You got any brothers named Mars and Venus? Hahahaha!"

Jupiter smiled weakly. Finally he was meeting the last of the five starting basketball players. Tim had cut every one of his classes last week, so Jupe hadn't been able to track him down. Now Jupe took in the whole picture. Tim was wearing expensive-looking clothes and bragging about buying all the beer. Maybe he was another player on Michael Anthony's payroll.

"You mean you bought *all* the beer for this party yourself?" Jupe asked.

"You got that straight, Jack. If you want to have friends, you gotta spend some money on them—am I right or am I right?" Tim held up his hand for a high-five, but he couldn't hold it steadily.

"Oh, you're right," Jupe said, slapping the big hand. "If you've got the money." He smiled at Sarah as if he were just making conversation.

"I've got all I need," Tim said with a goofy grin. "So, Jupe, buddy, what's your sport?"

"Uh, my major is—" Jupe wanted to say his major

was taking chances, because he knew he was about to take a big one. But with Tim's brain swimming around, it was an opportunity Jupe couldn't resist. "It's communications history," Jupe said. "I'm studying the history of television, old TV shows. One of my favorites is *The Millionaire*."

"Never heard of it," Tim said.

"It had a character named Michael Anthony." Jupe watched Tim's face carefully—and he wasn't disappointed.

"A show with Michael Anthony? For real?" Tim said with a laugh. "Hey, I'll bet that show had a lot of *Gravy Train* commercials." Tim laughed again, almost losing his balance.

"I don't get the joke," Jupe said. He was close. Jupe felt it. Just a little shove more and Tim Frisch would open up.

But just then Cory Brand came over to join the conversation.

"Hey, Cory, here's a joke. You'll like it," Tim said. "There's this TV show with a guy named Michael Anthony. And I said I bet it's got a lot of Gravy Train commercials. You get it, don't you? Jupiter doesn't get it. He doesn't get it at all."

Cory didn't laugh. His face got serious fast. "Come on, Tim," he said, pulling the big guy away from Jupe. "You've had too much to drink. You need some air."

"I didn't get it either," said Sarah.

"Must be a private joke," Jupe said, watching the evidence he almost had in his hands slip away.

"Telephone for Pete Crenshaw!" someone was shouting. "Yo! Pete Crenshaw! Is he here?"

Jupe watched Pete move through the crowd toward the guy with the phone.

"Well, Jupiter, are you going to ask me to dance?" Sarah said.

"Huh?" Jupe said. Suddenly his mind was split in two. Half of it wanted to dance with Sarah so badly he'd do anything—even go on the One-Quarter Diet if that would help. But the other half of his mind was watching Pete head for the phone. Who would be calling him—*here*?

Sarah saw the faraway look on Jupe's face and said, "Well, I guess you're not interested." Before Jupe could recover, she had walked away.

A moment later Pete came back to the living room, motioning for Jupe to join him.

"I just got a phone call," Pete said. "Some guy gave me a warning. He said, 'It's not safe to snoop around other people's business.' "

"Was the voice familiar?"

"Nope. He also said if I wanted to see what he meant, go look out the window."

Jupe and Pete hurried out onto the balcony. Just as they reached the railing there was a huge booming fireball explosion—coming from a car on the street.

"*Oh, no! My Porsche!*" Pete shouted.

12

Arresting Developments

PETE WATCHED THE BALL OF FIRE TURN INTO A cloud of black smoke. Pieces of the blue Porsche fell from the air. People on the street were running for cover.

Miraculously, no one had gotten hurt. But Jupe's heart was pounding as if he had just barely escaped with his life.

"Call the police." Jupe delivered it like an order, partly to steady his own nerves and partly to snap his friend out of his dazed stare. "Call the police, Pete!"

But Pete didn't move. And people inside Cory Brand's condo came rushing out onto the balcony to see what the noise was.

Jupe pushed his way back inside to call the cops himself. Cory's apartment was in Rocky Beach, so Jupe knew the phone number by heart. How many times had Jupe called the police to ask for help in a case? Zillions. But he'd *never* had to report a car bombing before—not of Pete's own car, anyway! He hurried back to Pete as soon as he hung up.

Pete was still staring, his hands gripping the balcony railing. Fire engines had arrived. The firefighters scrambled around, connecting hoses and squirting foam. Jupe's stomach turned over when he saw how long the fire burned—and how hard it was to extinguish the flames.

The doorbell rang and Jupe saw a Rocky Beach police officer come into the condo.

"Hey—we weren't making any noise," Cory Brand said the minute the officer stepped in.

The officer surveyed the party scene. "Someone here phoned to report that car bombing."

"That was I," Jupe said. He spoke over the general mumbles of the group as he stepped from the balcony back into the living room.

"I'd like to speak to you," said the officer, motioning Jupe toward the front doorway for a private conference.

Jupe tapped Pete, who still looked dazed, and got him to follow.

"I'm Jupiter Jones and this is my friend Pete Crenshaw. That's his car that was blown up," Jupe said, his voice cracking slightly on the last sentence.

"Do you have the registration?" the officer asked Pete.

"Well, no . . ." Pete looked at Jupe for help. But before Jupe could explain, the officer took two pairs of handcuffs from a pouch on his belt.

"Hold out your hands, boys," the officer said.

"Why? Hey, wait a minute. Jupe can explain!" Pete said.

The officer grabbed Jupe's wrists and clamped on the cuffs.

"Wait a—ow!—what are you doing? This is absurd," Jupe sputtered. "Do you know who you're dealing with?"

"Yeah—you're one of the Three Investigators, aren't you?" the officer sneered.

Jupe pulled himself up to his full height.

"I am a personal friend of Chief Reynolds," Jupe said, trying to maintain his composure. "Is this what you do when citizens report an incident?"

"This is what we do when we're bringing in suspects," said the officer as he roughly grabbed and cuffed Pete.

Suspects? Jupe thought. Suspects? "That's ridiculous. We didn't blow up that car! Where's your evidence?" Jupe demanded.

"I'm taking you in on suspicion of auto theft," said the officer. "We'll talk about it at the station."

When they got to the police station, the cuffs were finally taken off. The two friends sat next to each other on a hard wooden bench outside Police Chief Reynolds's office.

Pete stared at the floor and shifted uncomfortably. He felt like he was living a nightmare. "We could have been killed," he said.

"I know," Jupe said, his stomach turning over again.

"I don't think we were intended to die. But we might have been killed accidentally. It's clear we haven't been careful enough. Someone knew we were going to be at that party."

"But if they didn't want to kill us, why blow up the car?"

"To scare us," Jupe said. "Obviously we are getting close to something—too close."

Just then the door to Police Chief Reynolds's office opened. Officer Klimt, the cop who'd picked up the guys, motioned them in.

"Hello, Chief," said Jupiter as he entered.

"Jupiter. Pete," said the burly, balding man behind the desk. He was half hidden by a mess of files and notes and notepads.

"Chief," said Jupiter as if speaking to an old friend. Which of course he was. The Rocky Beach police chief had helped the Three Investigators a number of times. And vice versa. Bob liked to say they were "partners in crime-solving." So Jupe was startled to be hauled in like a common thief. "Why the use of handcuffs?" Jupe asked.

"Jupe," said the chief in a surprisingly unfriendly voice. "*I'm* going to do all the questioning for once." Suddenly he smiled pleasantly. "Well, Pete—that's quite a car."

It seemed like he was changing the subject, but Jupe knew Chief Reynolds too well. He knew his interrogation techniques. Make the suspect comfortable. Talk about something easy, gain his confidence—then spring the trap. But why was he using his techniques on Pete and Jupe?

"Yeah, it sure was," Pete said. "And maybe you should be out looking for the joker who blew it up."

"Pete," snapped the chief, "mind your manners. I know my job. Let's get down to the nitty-gritty. How long have you had that car?"

"Since Friday," Jupe answered because Pete was biting a fingernail.

"How'd you boys get it?"

"A man gave it to me," Pete answered.

Chief Reynolds crossed his arms and sniffed. "I don't like that answer," he said. Then he leaned forward with his elbows on his desk. "Try again."

"What do you want me to say?" Pete asked. "It followed me home? I told you the truth."

"All right, Pete. I've known you boys a long time, and I'm inclined to believe you. But there's more than one side to the truth here. The other side is that that car was reported stolen this afternoon."

"Stolen?" Pete said.

"By whom?" asked Jupe.

"By its owner. Barry Norman," said the chief.

"Barry Norman, why that's the—" Pete started to say. But Jupe interrupted him loudly.

"Pete, I think it's time to tell Chief Reynolds that we're working on a case and that that car was a part of it, and that we can't expose our client, *right*?"

"What? Oh, yeah, right," Pete said.

"What case?" asked Chief Reynolds.

Jupe shook his head. "I can't tell you," he said. "We've promised our client that we'd protect his interests by keeping this quiet."

The chief threw up his hands.

"If you keep me in the dark, I've got to go by the rule book, boys," said the chief.

"So do we," Jupe said.

They stared at each other for a long, tense minute. The chief was obviously upset.

"Bring in Norman," the chief finally said to Officer Klimt.

When the door opened again, Barry Norman walked in. As soon as they saw him, both Pete and Jupe gasped. Norman was Michael Anthony!

He was wearing a business suit with his shirt collar open and necktie loose. And his sunglasses hung around his neck on a red cord. Everything about Barry Norman—a.k.a. Michael Anthony—was cool and relaxed. But he looked at Jupe and Pete with a gaze so intense it practically burned holes in their eye sockets. Then he blinked and looked at them again as if he had never seen them before.

"Mr. Norman," said Chief Reynolds, "these are the boys who reported that your car was blown up. I can vouch for their character. I've known them all their lives. Their story is they've been driving your Porsche since Friday, when someone gave it to them."

"I suppose that's possible," Barry Norman said coolly. "My car could have been missing for longer than I thought. I've been away on a business trip. Perhaps whoever stole it decided to give it away—although I can't imagine why."

"Have you ever seen Pete or Jupiter before?"

Barry Norman slowly shook his head.

"And Jupiter, you refuse to tell me who your client is?"

Jupe's mind raced through the possibilities like a high-speed computer. He could see that Barry Norman was doing the same thing.

The bottom line, Jupe decided, was that Barry Norman was a small catch. By his own admission, he worked for someone who wanted to remain anonymous. But who? If Jupe blew this case open by telling Chief Reynolds about it, chances were good that the man behind the scheme would quietly disappear.

"We can't tell you anything right now," Jupe replied.

"Client? Are these kids detectives or something?" Barry Norman asked, trying very hard to look unconcerned.

"Darned good ones," answered the chief.

"How's that for a surprise?" Pete said.

Norman shrugged. "The world is full of surprises," he said. "Sometimes you get a break and sometimes your car blows up."

"So do you want to file charges against them, Mr. Norman?" asked the chief.

"No," said Barry Norman. "I think you're right,

Chief Reynolds. These guys didn't blow up my car. Now I've got to go try to explain this to my insurance agent."

"I'll be in touch," said Chief Reynolds.

Norman walked out. After he was gone, the chief leaned back in his chair. "I should make you two hotshots tell me the whole story," he said.

"You'd only get half the story if you did that, Chief," Jupe said. "We're still writing the conclusion."

"Jupiter," the chief said, "you guys better be careful. Ve-ry careful. Someone who blows away a $45,000 car doesn't care about happy endings!"

13

Personal Fouls

MICHAEL ANTHONY WAS BARRY NORMAN! PETE still couldn't get over that fact. Even now, Wednesday night, almost 24 hours later, the case didn't quite make sense to him. All he knew was that he agreed with Jupe: Barry Norman was a dangerous guy—someone they should steer clear of for a few days. Let him think they were off the case. Then maybe he'd get sloppy and let a clue drop.

Pete sat in the back of the Rocky Beach High School bus by himself, letting his mind wander. Sometimes he tried to put the pieces of the case together. Sometimes he just focused on the upcoming basketball game. His legs were stretched out on the seat, the back of his head bumping on the window to the jerky motion of the bus.

The rest of the Rocky Beach basketball team rode up front. They were talking and laughing and trying to blow off some nerves before that night's game. But they were leaving Pete alone because that's what he said he wanted.

Everyone on the bus had heard one story or another about Pete's Porsche being blown to bits. They had a million questions, but they weren't asking them.

Pete took deep breaths, trying to relax completely so he'd be loose for the game. It was weird playing a basketball game in the middle of winter break. But that's the way the schedule had worked out and Pete didn't mind. He was glad for the chance to get away from the case—away from homicidal college jocks and strange phone calls and exploding cars.

Everyone thinks I'm mad about losing the Porsche, Pete thought.

But he wasn't as upset about that as he was about Chief Reynolds chewing him out. And the warning. The warning from the chief had freaked him. Because the chief was right. This case had suddenly gotten dangerous. Really dangerous.

That's why he was sitting in the back of the bus doing deep-breathing exercises. He was trying to make the fear go away.

The bus finally pulled into the Wolfford High School parking lot. As the team filed into the visitors' locker room, Coach Tong called Pete aside. "Are you okay, Pete? Can you start tonight?" he asked. "And don't give me a quick answer. Four other guys, your teammates, need you to tell me the absolute truth right now."

"Coach, I'm totally ready," Pete said.

Coach Tong smiled for a second. "That's what I wanted to hear," he said. "Get dressed."

The locker room was a typical visitors' locker room—small, dark, and either too cold or too hot depending on which would make the players more uncomfortable. Pete sat down on a wooden bench that needed a good sanding and jerked open the door of a banged-up old metal locker.

And all of a sudden his heart started pounding—*thumpa, thumpa, thumpa*—like a hard basketball on a new gym floor. There was an envelope lying on the rusty bottom inside. Another envelope!

For an instant Pete wanted to slam the door closed. But he didn't. He picked up the envelope, opened it, and unfolded the note inside. It said:

"Forget about the Shoremont case. It's none of your business. Otherwise you could get hurt REAL BAD—like you will tonight. And you'll never play basketball again."

Pete's pulse was racing and his lungs were trying to keep up. He kicked the locker closed. "Who put this in my locker?" he shouted. He had everyone's attention immediately. "Come on. Who did it?"

"Hey, Pete, what's the problem?" asked Bill Konkey. "I put it in there."

Pete stormed over to Bill's locker and stood over him. "Why?" he demanded.

"Some guy outside gave it to me and said it was from Kelly. I know you always use the locker that matches your basketball number, so I stuck it in there. What's the problem?"

Pete got a chill. He looked at the note again. Was

it the same typewriter as before? Was it from Michael Anthony? Did he really know who Kelly was?

Coach Tong stuck his head inside the locker room. "What's going on? Are you guys waiting for an invitation? Let's play basketball!"

Pete tossed the letter into the locker and hurried to dress for the game.

A few minutes later the Rocky Beach team ran onto the court. The gym was filled with a raucous mixture of sounds: cheers for the Wolfford team, the Wolfford band playing their fight song at triple speed, scattered boos for the Rocky Beach players when they hit the court, and the game announcer warming up and testing the PA microphone. Over it all, a small traveling section of the Rocky Beach marching band was struggling to be heard.

It was the kind of chaos that normally got Pete really pumped up for the game and the competition. But tonight it just intensified his fear. Right now what he needed more than anything in the world was to forget about the case, relax, and play ball. But how could he? Someone was out there waiting to hurt him. Who?

Pete looked at the crowd, an ocean of unfamiliar faces. The noise in the gym seemed to get louder every second, but Pete heard only one thing. "You could get hurt REAL BAD—like you will tonight." The words of the note pounded in his head.

Okay, Pete thought, getting tough. They can try to take me out, but I'm going out fighting!

In the next instant the Wolfford team came out, and the game was under way.

Wolfford was a tall team. Every player was taller than Pete. And they controlled the tip, moving quickly toward the Rocky Beach basket. But their shooting was cold. A miss. A miss on the rebound.

Rocky Beach took the ball. A long pass from Valdez to Bill Konkey got the ball across midcourt. Konkey kept looking to pass to Pete, but a Wolfford player named Traut was all over him. Traut kept holding Pete with a hand to his chest, pushing Pete from the side.

Pete faked a move one way and then moved the other way around Traut. Konkey saw that Pete was open and passed him the ball. But suddenly Pete crashed to the floor, banging his elbow and landing on his other hand. The ball went sailing out of bounds. Wolfford's ball.

Pete was furious. Traut had tripped him, but no one saw it. "Watch it," he snapped at Traut.

"I'm watching you," the lanky player said.

As the game went on, more things started to happen. And Pete quickly realized that Traut was the heavy who was going to hurt him real bad. Pete tried to avoid Traut, but he had to play ball—and Traut was clearly out to kill him.

First Pete got an elbow in the eye and sat out for a few minutes with an ice pack on the side of his face. When he went back in, he got shoved off the court on a fast break lay-up. Pete ended up sprawled on someone's lap in the crowd, his head bleeding from hitting the bleachers.

Nine of the guys were out there to play basketball. But Traut was out there for one thing only: to destroy Pete.

It made Pete so mad he played harder, moving, twisting, making fakes and then impossible shots while flying through the air. Rocky Beach was ahead, but it was a close game all the way.

Thumpa, thumpa, thumpa. Traut was dribbling across the center stripe. Pete picked him up, guarding him, moving with him, blocking him from getting close enough to take a shot.

"You're taking a lot of chances. Get smart," Traut said to him. "It's going to get worse."

I'll get smart, all right, Pete thought. *"Hiii-ya!"* he shouted at the top of his lungs. It broke Traut's concentration just long enough for Pete to slap the ball. He stole it away and fired a pass to Konkey, who scored. But as soon as the officials weren't looking, Traut gave Pete an elbow in the back, right in the kidneys.

Pain shot through Pete like an electric charge. But he wasn't going to show it—not for a second. "Kiss me again, sweetheart," he told Traut, glaring at him.

On a rebound the ball came sailing back into Traut's hands, and without pausing a second, he dribbled down the court and leaped into the air.

The ball sank and Traut said with a grunt, "There's your kiss—sweetheart."

The game stayed close and tough. It was tied at 48

going into the final five minutes. Traut threw a pass that hit Pete in the back of the head. To everyone else it looked like a bad pass. But Pete knew it was a direct hit, another reminder from Michael Anthony—or someone else—to get off the case.

With less than a minute left Coach Tong called a time-out, the team's last. "Sit down, Pete."

"No way," Pete said. "Traut's been after me all night. He's trying to hurt me. I can't let him get away with it."

"I've seen good aggressive basketball, not a hitman," said the coach. "Don't make this personal or I'll yank you."

Pete nodded and huddled up.

"Okay, we're up by two," said Coach Tong. "Now—pressure defense, no cheap fouls, and don't give them an easy basket."

The team clasped hands and charged back onto the court.

But as soon as play resumed, Pete knew that Wolfford wasn't ready to roll over and play dead. Wolfford threw the ball upcourt and scored an easy lay-up to tie the game. Then they stole the ball right back from Rocky Beach, and held it. They were eating up the clock and trying to take the last shot.

"Stay cool! Stay cool!" Bill Konkey shouted to the team.

Finally, with only seconds left to play, a Wolfford player took a shot at the basket and missed. Konkey got the rebound and passed it to Pete.

The crowd was going nuts, screaming the count-down. Time was almost out. "Three . . . two . . ." Pete dribbled, but there was no time to pass. So he went for a desperation move. He leaped into the air and heaved the ball sidearm as hard as he could.

And then to his utter amazement he watched the ball smash into the backboard, bounce off the front rim of the basket, and—somehow—drop through the hoop! The buzzer rang before anyone could believe their eyes. Pete had won the game from two feet past center court!

His team swarmed around him, pounding him, lift-ing him up and carrying him back to the locker room. The Wolfford crowd was still stunned silent. Pete wanted to find Traut, to get in his face, but he was carried away too fast.

The victory celebration was going to go on all night, but Pete didn't want any part of it. All he wanted was to shower quickly and then go find Traut. He waited for him in the dark parking lot outside the gym.

"Hey," he said when Traut came out.

For a moment Traut looked surprised.

"What's your problem?" Pete asked. "Who told you to come after me?"

Traut said nothing and glared at Pete.

"Come on, buddy. No officials, no time-outs now," Pete said. "So you tell me what was going on in there, or I'll show you the real meaning of the words 'per-sonal foul'!"

"Bug off," Traut said. He shoved Pete into some cars and tried to get past him.

Pete bounced back and shoved Traut. Recovering quickly, Traut threw a punch that caught Pete right in the gut.

For an instant Pete could hardly breathe. The wind was knocked out of him. It only lasted an instant, though. Then he flew into action.

"*Hi-yaaaaa!*" Pete karate-kicked Traut, sending him flying onto his back on the hood of a car. Traut kicked back, his legs flailing like a child's. Pete grabbed Traut's ankles, yanked him forward, and then threw him over his left shoulder in one smooth, twisting motion.

Nothing like knowing karate, Pete thought as he looked at Traut lying on the ground. None of Traut's tough-guy moves, now or during the game, could stand up to the karate skills Pete had developed over the years. Traut knew it, too, because he just lay there, even though he wasn't really very hurt. He *could* get up, but he didn't want to.

"Okay," Pete said. "Now tell me. Who told you to do a number on me? Come on, slimeball. The truth!"

"I don't know," Traut said weakly.

Pete reached down and jerked Traut up by his shirt. "The truth!"

"I don't know, I swear. The guy wouldn't tell me his name. Not his real name, anyway," Traut said. "He just gave me two hundred bucks and told me to rough you up during the game. And he gave me a letter to deliver to you. I didn't even read it."

"What do you mean, 'not his real name'?" Pete demanded, giving Traut a yank to put him back on his feet.

"I mean he gave me a phony name. He admitted it," Traut said.

"What was it?" Pete asked.

"Michael Anthony."

14

Photo Opportunity

VERY LATE THAT NIGHT JUPE, BOB, AND PETE SAT IN the crowded fluorescent-light fantasy of Hank's 24-Hour One-Stop, one of Rocky Beach's more unusual hangouts.

Pete was hunched over a soda and Hank's sandwich of the night. After midnight the sandwich was free with an extra-large soda, but it was made of leftovers from the day shift. Tonight it was a meatloaf and tuna salad combo.

While he ate, Pete told Bob and Jupe about the Wolfford game, Traut's vicious attacks, and the karate fight in the parking lot. Then he drank all 32 ounces of his soda in one gulp.

"I was parched," he told Jupe.

"Dehydrated," Jupe corrected. "You lost a lot of fluid in perspiration during the game. I know how you feel."

"Oh, yeah, that's right," Pete said with a laugh. "You were the parrot at the Shoremont game tonight. Did you learn anything new?"

Jupe shook his head glumly.

"Forget the case for a few minutes, okay?" Bob said. "We're here to celebrate Pete's big win!"

"This place is definitely beyond weird," Pete said, looking around Hank's. "Why is almost everyone wearing black?"

"It's Wednesday, Pete," explained Bob. "It's one of Hank's deals. Wear black on Wednesday, you get a ten percent discount."

"How do you know so much about this place?" Pete asked.

"I've been here after late-night recording sessions," Bob said. "That's when I found out it's the best place to wait for the first edition of the morning paper. It'll be here by two in the A.M. Hank guarantees it."

"You really think there'll be a story about me in the paper?" asked Pete.

"Don't get your hopes up," Jupe said, yawning. "It's a long shot, Pete."

"Don't listen to him," Bob said. "I'm telling you, Pete, if your winning basket was only half as long as you say it was, it will make the papers. It's too good not to."

"I think the most *notable* event of the evening was the *note* in Pete's locker," said Jupe.

Bob and Pete groaned.

"Well, the note was interesting to me because it signals that Barry Norman is still trying to scare us off the case," said Jupe. "He knows we're closing in on him."

"Not fast enough," Pete said, returning with another large soda. "I want to get that guy off the streets."

"That would be easy with what we know about him already," Jupe said. "But President Harper wants us to find the man Barry Norman is working for. A task at which we have so far failed."

"Hey, whatever happened to the old it's-not-over-till-it's-over Jupiter Jones?" asked Bob.

Jupe put his head down on the table. "I've been jumping around in a parrot costume all night. I'm exhausted! I can't solve a case with no sleep," he moaned. "We should be going home, not waiting here for the newspaper."

"We won't have to wait much longer," said Bob, pointing to the door. "The papers are here."

Bob got up and hurried to join the line at the cash register to buy a newspaper. Bob went because Hank was so weird that he sometimes insisted that people line up alphabetically. Andrews was the best last name among the three of them.

"Hey, Jupe, are you going to eat the other half of your meatloaf-tuna sandwich?" Pete asked.

Jupe pushed his plate over to Pete. "Sometimes I think if I weren't on a diet, you'd starve."

"Hey, Pete. They didn't just write a little story about you," Bob said, dropping an open newspaper onto the table. "It's the headline story. 'Long Shot Wins Game.' "

"Wow! Look!" Pete said, grabbing the newspaper away. "It's even got a photo of me!"

There was a picture across the top of the page taken by a photographer who must have been standing high up in the bleachers. The photo showed the whole court, with Pete standing on the far side of midcourt. Everyone was watching the ball, which had been frozen in midair.

" 'For the second game in a row,' " Pete said, reading from the article, " 'Rocky Beach guard Pete Crenshaw showed that small guys on the court can win big. This time Pete's game-winning shot came with no time on the clock and about 40 feet between him and the basket.' " Pete turned the newspaper around and pointed at the picture. "Pretty cool, huh? Hey, you're looking at the wrong picture, Jupe."

Jupe snatched the paper out of Pete's hands so he could study a photo at the bottom of the page. "Look at this," he said finally. "See if you recognize anyone."

Pete folded the newspaper page in half and looked at the smaller photo at the bottom of the page. "It's a story about the Shoremont basketball team," he said. "And the picture shows a bunch of Shoremont players on the bench during a game."

"In the background," Jupe hinted impatiently.

Bob moved to look at the photo over Pete's shoulder. But Pete quickly pulled the newspaper away. "Don't help me," he told Bob. "I'm going to get this one myself."

Pete leaned on both elbows and stared closely at the newspaper photo. Finally his eyebrows lifted in recognition. "That's the woman Barry Norman had lunch with at the country club. And she's sitting with John Hemingway Powers."

"Right," Jupe said, "so now we know that she knows both Barry Norman and John Hemingway Powers. Now here's an interesting scenario: If she knows both those guys, isn't it possible that they know each other? That would mean we have a new suspect, a new clue, a new lead."

Pete scrunched his face. "Powers?"

"Okay, okay," Jupe said. "I'll grant you this: It's another long shot. But maybe there's a reason why we haven't found anything that connects Barry Norman with Coach Duggan. Maybe it's because there *isn't* anything. But now we've got a real link between Norman and Powers."

Bob cleared his throat. "Come on, guys. Would you let me in on this? Hand over the newspaper." Pete passed it to Bob, who took a long look at the photo. "What did you say his name was?"

"John Hemingway Powers," said Jupe. "He's the super-bucks alumnus of Shoremont College we told you about a few days ago."

"And he's the one who was putting all the pressure on you to nail Duggan?" asked Bob.

"You should have seen him," Pete said.

"I *have* seen him," Bob said, smiling.

"You have? When? Where?" Jupe asked.

"Remember last week when I met you in the Shoremont gym? I was hanging around in Duggan's office, talking to his secretary. I told you people were in and out of there a lot. Well, he was one of them. I didn't think it was important at the time, so I just filed it."

"What exactly happened?" asked Jupe.

"He came in, headed straight for Duggan's private office, and closed the door. I asked Duggan's secretary what was going on and she said he does it every week—usually on Thursdays when Duggan's not in. She said he uses Duggan's computer to get a printout of the latest statistics from the game. I got the message he's a *real* fan—in other words, fanatic about the team."

"Powers comes in and uses Coach Duggan's computer?" asked Pete.

"When he's not there. You got it," Bob said. "Are you thinking what I'm thinking?"

Jupe nodded. "If Powers goes into Duggan's office for the stats—what's to stop him from also getting copies of Duggan's scouting reports? He reads the reports, checks them out to see who Duggan wants for the team—"

"And then," finished Pete, "Powers tells Michael Anthony a.k.a. Barry Norman to send out a bribe."

"That would explain how Powers connected so quickly with Pete," Jupe added. "He knew Pete was at the top of Duggan's list, so he sent Michael Anthony to deliver the first envelope. We concluded that Coach Duggan left it because he happened to speak to Pete that same night."

"But we were wrong," Pete said.

"We weren't wrong," said Jupe, tapping the newspaper. "We were hasty. Do you think Hank would sell me half a black-and-white milk shake?"

"I thought you were dead tired," said Pete.

"I am. But I'm going to need the shake to revive. Because it's going to take a while to explain my plan for catching John Hemingway Powers!"

•   •   •

Jupe's plan was simple. They would set a trap for John Hemingway Powers by planting some bait in Coach Duggan's latest scouting report—and hope that Powers fell for it. Luckily the next day was Thursday, the day that Powers usually came into the office for the game statistics.

Early the next morning the Three Investigators went to Shoremont College and zeroed in on Coach Duggan's office.

Jupe and Pete hid in a janitor's closet across the hall. While they watched through a crack in the door, Bob poked his head into the office. "Hi. Remember me?" he said, pouring on the charm for Coach Duggan's secretary.

"Don't tell me you're still lost," she said.

"No—lost again," Bob said.

Once again the blonde offered to point Bob in the right direction, but this time Bob got her to walk with him part of the way, leaving the office unoccupied. As soon as they were gone Pete and Jupe sneaked into the inner office and headed straight for Coach Duggan's computer.

Jupe had it up and running in seconds.

"I'm into Coach Duggan's scouting reports now," Jupe said, his fingers flying on the keyboard. As he typed, entering information, a smile broke across his face.

"What's so funny?" Pete asked, taking his eyes off the doorway for only a second.

"Tell you later. I'm almost done." Jupe finished typing and then exited the program. "It's in there. Step one completed. Let's go."

They ran back into the closet, where they hid and waited, hoping Powers would come.

Two hours later Powers arrived. As Bob had reported, he went into Duggan's office and emerged a few minutes later with a computer printout.

"There goes the bait," Jupe said. "Powers has used the computer. And Duggan hasn't been in his office all morning. Step two completed. Now it's time for step three. Good luck, Pete. Sorry I can't go with you, but it's too risky. I might be recognized as the parrot. Make it quick—and make sure you go in there alone."

Pete stepped out of the closet carrying a clipboard in his hand and a pen behind his ear. He walked across the hall.

"Can I help you?" asked Duggan's secretary, sitting at her desk sipping a can of diet soda.

"Computer maintenance," Pete said, tapping the clipboard with the pen. "Gotta check it out."

"Coach has one," she said. "I'll show you."

"No. I mean, thanks. But—uh—I'll find it."

"Okay," said the young woman.

Pete went into the back office and sat down at the computer. Sweat instantly beaded on his forehead. A car he could take apart and stick back together blindfolded. Computers were a different animal. His hands trembled as he typed on the keyboard. Delete . . . delete . . . He checked and double-checked Jupe's instructions on his clipboard.

When Pete was finished, he left Duggan's inner office, thanked the secretary, and walked into the hall. A quick, quiet knock on the closet door brought Jupe out.

"You did it?" Jupe asked.

Pete nodded. "I deleted all of the stuff you just put in."

"Good. Step three completed. Now we just have to wait for someone to contact Luke Braun—even though he doesn't exist!"

15

The Game Is Over

"OKAY, TELL US EVERYTHING ABOUT THE FICTItious Luke Braun," Bob said, driving back to Rocky Beach.

"You mean everything I made up for the scouting report?" said Jupe. He had a look of pure smugness on his face. "For starters, Luke Braun is a straight-A student."

"Always important to a basketball coach," Bob said, rolling his eyes.

"It's important to me, and I created him." Jupe bristled. "He's six feet six inches tall."

"That's more like it," said Pete.

"He has a remarkable shooting percentage, he's completely ambidextrous—I thought that was an interesting touch—and I wrote that he was fast, slim, and agile. I also added that Coach Duggan thought Luke was destined to become the next Magic Johnson."

"Wow!" Pete said. "Hey, if I were a coach, I'd sign that kid up no matter what."

"That's the idea. To make Powers salivate to recruit him for Shoremont. I also added that Luke was going to decide by today what college to attend. Of course since Luke doesn't exist, I gave him your phone number and address, Bob. Now we just have to wait at your house for the phone to ring."

In the middle of the afternoon the right call finally came. Bob answered and immediately pointed at the receiver to signal Jupe and Pete that this was it.

"Yes, this is Luke Braun," Bob said, taking the phone and sitting down sideways in a large stuffed living room chair.

Jupe could tell from the smile on Bob's face that the phone call was going exactly as planned. First Bob acted interested in talking to Michael Anthony—but then he began to set the trap.

"Sure, I want to talk to you. But I'm not comfortable meeting you someplace. My parents and I decided that I wouldn't meet with anyone except here at my house and with them. My dad just lost his job, and we don't have much money. They're very eager for me to find a college that can help out."

Bob listened some more and finally gave Pete and Jupe a thumbs-up. "Great," he said, and hung up the phone. "E.T.A.—one hour."

When the doorbell rang about an hour later, Bob answered it.

"Hi, you must be Michael Anthony," said Bob, opening the door. "I'm Luke."

Barry Norman came in and sat down, but he was

looking at Bob quizzically. "The scouting report said you're six six."

"I do some fantastic stretching exercises before each game," Bob said.

The answer obviously didn't sit well with Barry Norman. He squirmed in his chair. "You *are* Luke Braun?"

"Sure. Some people think I'm the next Magic Johnson," said Bob. "Can we talk money now, Mr. Anthony, because I've got three other schools coming over to bribe me this afternoon."

Barry Norman's face remained calm as his eyes surveyed every inch of the room. "I think I'll be going, Luke."

Bob stood up before Norman could move. "Wait!" he said. "I want you to meet my mom and dad before you go. They're really eager to say hello, especially since they've made me what I am today. Hey, guys!"

At that signal Pete and Jupe walked into the living room. They were delighted to see Barry Norman's face, already confused, go pale.

"Good afternoon, Mr. Norman," said Jupe. "We forgot to tell you in Chief Reynolds' office that we are the *Three* Investigators. This is Bob Andrews, our third associate." Jupe could not conceal his triumphant smile. "I also want to thank you for coming, Mr. Norman, because by showing up today, you have just proved who is behind the bribery scheme at Shoremont College."

"No, I haven't. And if you think I'm going to incriminate someone, you're very naive."

"You already did incriminate someone," said Bob, "when you called me."

"You see, Mr. Norman," Jupe explained, "there is only one way you could have learned about Luke Braun and gotten his phone number. And that is if John Hemingway Powers told you. Because Luke Braun doesn't exist."

Jupe sat down on a couch two feet away from Barry Norman's chair. The two stared at each other for a long time.

"I'm making no admission of any guilt, you understand," Norman finally said. "But if I were working for John Hemingway Powers, so what? I haven't done anything illegal, and for that matter neither has John Hemingway Powers."

"That may be true," Jupe said. "But I can't imagine that your law practice will benefit from all the negative publicity when this news reaches the press. On the other hand, if you cooperate, President Harper might agree to keep you out of it."

Norman's face was as cold as stone, his voice even colder.

"I see no reason why I can't attend a meeting with Harper, if that's what you want," he said at last.

•   •   •

Jupe beamed the whole time he was climbing into Bob's red VW and riding to the Shoremont campus.

He had already phoned President Harper to tell him
the case was solved. He asked Harper to summon
Coach Duggan to his office and to invite John Hemingway Powers as well. Now the Three Investigators
were driving to Shoremont, with Barry Norman following them in his own car.

When they arrived at Harper's office, Duggan and
Powers were already there.

The college president greeted and shook hands with
each of the Three Investigators, but Jupe barely paid
attention to him. He was too busy watching John Hemingway Powers's reaction as Barry Norman walked in
the door behind the three teenagers. Surprise, anger,
fear, puzzlement, and belligerence all passed over the
man's face. Then he stared hard at the Investigators.

"Jupiter," said President Harper, "we're all very eager to hear what you've learned. You three must be
very good detectives to have solved this case in just two
weeks—and you have my gratitude. Now please tell us
what you've found."

"Detectives? I'm missing something," grumbled
Coach Duggan from his chair by the window. "I don't
see detectives. I see our school parrot and"—he
pointed at Pete—"a high school kid."

Jupe stepped to the center of the room. "In fact, all
three of us are detectives *and* high school students,
Coach Duggan," he explained. "I have only been posing as a Shoremont student."

"Coach," said President Harper, "you'll understand
in a minute. Come on, Jupiter. Tell us."

Jupe was not in a hurry. He thought of John Hemingway Powers as a chestnut: very hard nut, with a shell impossible to peel off—unless you roasted it first. Once Powers was hot enough, worried enough, Jupe hoped he would crack.

"It was a difficult case to solve," Jupe said. "Some things came easily. For example, this man, Barry Norman, offered Pete money and a Porsche to play basketball for Shoremont College."

"What?" shouted the coach.

"Don't interrupt, Duggan," said President Harper sternly. "You'll have your chance to explain in a minute."

Everyone in the room could hear that President Harper was accusing Coach Duggan. Powers let a small smile creep into the corners of his mouth.

"I'm afraid you've jumped to a wrong conclusion," Jupe told the college president. "We're certain now that Coach Duggan is entirely innocent in this matter."

"Well, then, who *is* guilty?" Harper was losing his patience.

"I'll tell you in just a moment, but first let me ask Mr. Powers just one question," Jupe said. "Mr. Powers, who is Luke Braun?"

Powers looked at Jupe cautiously.

"Who is Luke Braun?" Powers repeated.

"Yes," Jupe said. "You know who he is, don't you?"

Powers thought a moment, trying to find the trap. But he obviously couldn't see it.

"Well, I think he's a high school basketball player," Powers said. "I've seen his name on Coach Duggan's scouting reports. He's supposed to be darned good."

Everyone looked at the quiet, sullen coach. "Luke Braun? Never heard of him," said Coach Duggan.

Powers looked confused. "But I saw your scouting report," he insisted. "You said he was the next Magic Johnson!"

"No," interrupted Jupe. "*I* said that. You see, Mr. Powers, Luke Braun doesn't exist. I made him up and entered his name in Coach Duggan's computer, knowing that you would read it. And knowing that you would send Michael Anthony—Barry Norman, here—to see him. We erased the file minutes after you left, Mr. Powers, so we know you were the only person who read the report. I'm afraid our proof is conclusive."

Powers's face looked suddenly tired and old.

"Is this true, Mr. Norman?" asked President Harper.

"I'd like to help you out here," Barry Norman said. "But first I need some assurances that my role in this matter will be kept confidential. I'd like to propose a deal. My cooperation in exchange for your promise to keep my name out of the media coverage of the story."

"Fine," President Harper said. "If that's the price of your information, I'm willing to pay it. Now tell me, are the Three Investigators right?"

Norman looked right at Powers and nodded. "Yes.

John Hemingway Powers has been my client. He's the one behind this bribery scheme."

"All right, it's true! So what?" Powers said almost proudly. "I don't happen to believe there's anything wrong with giving guys extra incentives to attend this fine school and join its basketball team."

President Harper's brow wrinkled as he scowled. "John, what you happen to believe is against every rule of college recruitment ethics."

"It's easy for you to sit up here and talk ethics," Powers said. "You've only been here three years. You didn't graduate from this school. You don't know the traditions and the history. You didn't see the good years. You didn't have to watch the athletic program dissolve into mediocrity, watch as year after year talented players chose the big schools with the big names and the big TV coverage of their games. There had to be some way for me to restore this school to what it was—I knew *you* weren't going to do it."

"How long has this been going on?" asked President Harper.

"Only since you hired Duggan," answered Powers. "The idea came to me when I heard the rumors about Duggan paying his players in Boston. Did I think it was true? I didn't care. All I knew was that it sounded like a great idea. One thing I know: Money talks and people listen. I figured if the payoffs were ever exposed, Duggan would take the blame."

"So that's why you offered me more money for

Duggan's budget," President Harper said. "Just to try to incriminate him further?"

"I had to, Chuck. When these kids started tailing Barry and asking my players lot of questions, I smelled trouble." Then Powers turned his fierce stare on Pete. "Who would have guessed we'd recruit a detective?"

Pete didn't know what to say.

"Powers, you're an egotist and an embarrassment to the sport." Duggan spat out the words.

"Wake up, Duggan," Powers said, snapping his fingers like a hypnotist. "Champion teams are *bought*, not coached! Our team is in the play-offs for the first time in a decade. And we can win. All of you should be thanking *me* for that."

President Harper looked so defeated that for a moment Jupe was almost sorry they'd solved the case.

"Well, Powers," Harper said sadly. "It's over."

"That's for sure," the coach chimed in. "I'm kicking every one of your pets off the team, Powers."

"Don't be absurd," Powers said. "The play-offs are tomorrow night. No one has to know about this."

"We may be the best team your money can buy, John," said President Harper, twisting a paper clip between his fingers, "but that's not how I want our athletic program run. And please don't tell me that you're withdrawing your financial support for the gym, because I wouldn't take any of your money now. This school has no use for you anymore."

Powers stood up to give everyone in the room one last stare. Then he marched out.

"Thanks, you guys," President Harper said, giving the Three Investigators a weak smile but a firm handshake. "This school is about to go through a tough, embarrassing time. But at least we'll be able to take some pride in exposing our problems and fixing them ourselves instead of covering them up."

16

MVP

"WELL, IT SOUNDS LIKE YOU HAD FUN WHILE I WAS skiing," said Kelly. "But come on, guys. Tell me the truth. There never was a Porsche, was there?"

Pete gripped the wheel of the Ark. After he abandoned the Cadillac at the scenic lookout a week ago, the police had towed it to an impoundment lot. It had cost Pete $80 to bail it out that morning—cash he really hated to lose since he'd already returned the $4000 in bribe money to Powers. Now the Ark was taking his friends to the Shoremont basketball play-off game. "I don't want to talk about the Porsche, okay?" Pete said.

"Okay," Kelly said, and waited a beat. "But just tell me why this Michael Anthony guy blew it up."

Pete groaned.

"John Powers probably had him pay someone to blow it up," corrected Jupe from the back seat. "It was really Powers' car to begin with."

"But why blow it up?"

"Because Barry Norman knew we were getting close to him," Jupe explained. "It was a totally avoidable mistake on our part. When we were tailing Barry Norman, we thought we were keeping our distance. However, when you're driving a $45,000 sports car and tailing the person who owns it, you have to stay back an *extra long* way. We just weren't careful enough. After the meeting yesterday, Norman admitted to me that he saw the car parked at his country club when we followed him. So he took us on a wild-goose chase."

"Really?" Pete said. "So *that's* why he drove to Costa Verde College—just to make us think maybe he was working for Bernie Mehl. I guess that's why he never called me that Saturday—when you made me stay home all day waiting, Jupe!"

"I'll bet he saw the car when you were parked near his office building, too," said Bob.

"Yes," Jupe said with a sigh. "Similar mistake, similar results. That's why Norman never showed up that afternoon. In fact, the whole time we were waiting for him, *he* was watching *us*. And busily dialing his friendly neighborhood explosives expert on his car phone, I suspect. Norman would never admit that he masterminded the car bombing. But I'm fairly certain he followed us to the party. Then some pyrotechnic genius planted the bomb, made the phone call to Pete, and pushed the button on a remote control. Pretty elaborate scare tactics, if you ask me."

"Over*kill*?" Bob asked.

"Ouch." Jupe winced.

"I like the romantic part about this case," Kelly said.

"What romantic part?" Pete said, looking confused.

"I mean the beautiful young woman having lunch with Barry Norman. And then she turned out to be John Powers' daughter! That's so . . . so . . . cinematic!"

"Yeah, well, according to what Norman told me yesterday," said Jupe, "there's going to be bloodshed when Powers finds out Norman has been dating his daughter. Especially since that's what tipped the whole case for us."

Pete pulled into a parking space in the Shoremont College parking garage. He quickly went around to Kelly's door and yanked it open on the second try.

"Maybe it just needs a little work on the hinges," Bob said encouragingly.

"Yeah, with a jackhammer," Pete moaned.

"Come on, you guys. The case is closed. And this game is going to be wild," Kelly said, trying to change the subject. She hustled the guys toward the front doors of the Shoremont gym.

But as they pushed through the crowd to their seats in the bleachers, Jupe and Bob continued to go over the details of the case.

"The most embarrassing part," Jupe admitted, "came yesterday toward the end of the meeting in Harper's office, when I told Duggan that Walt Klinglesmith was one of the guys on the take. It turns out I was wrong. Walt has a lot of money—and expensive pens—to throw around for a very good reason: His parents own a chain of stationery stores."

Bob laughed sympathetically.

"It's going to be a weird game tonight, I'll tell you that," said Pete. "With Cory Brand, Tim Frisch, and four other guys suspended, it's like Shoremont put its best chances to win on a bus."

"Yeah, and without Jupe as the parrot, school spirit is going to be a total washout, too," Bob chimed in.

"Jupiter Jones, don't tell me you quit just because the team's going to lose!" Kelly said indignantly. "That's against the cheerleaders' code!"

"He didn't quit. He was politely fired when they found out he was an impostor," Bob explained.

Finally the foursome found their seats—midway up in the bleachers and right at center court. Great seats, courtesy of Coach Duggan.

"Well, guys," Pete said as soon as Jupe sat down, "who's getting the dogs, the drinks, and the popcorn?"

"Will someone *split* a hot dog with me?" asked Jupe.

"You need a new diet," Bob said with a laugh.

Then suddenly Jupe saw the Shoremont cheerleaders warming up on the sidelines. "I'll go for the food," Jupe volunteered, quickly pushing his way against the traffic, heading back downstairs. When he got to the bottom, he stood staring at Sarah, rehearsing the words he had practiced about fifty times with Bob. "Would you like to go to the movies?" Eight words, seven of them with only one syllable. What was the problem? Jupe felt ready . . . sort of.

He waved to Sarah and she came over.

"Hi, Jupe," she said. She looked surprised to see him.

"Uh, hi. What do you think about the movies?" Sarah's pretty face turned puzzled.

Jupe cleared his throat. "I mean, you go to the movies, don't you? That is . . ." Eight words, seven with only one syllable. Why couldn't he say them?

"Jupiter, I want to thank you for helping the school and for being our parrot. Boy, when I heard that you're in high school and a detective, well, I thought, wow, what a surprise. And then I thought about it some more, and said, nothing would surprise me about Jupiter."

Jupe took a deep breath. "In that case, would you like to, uh . . ."

Sarah broke the silence. "Maybe when you get to college we'll run into each other sometimes." She smiled, touched his arm, and walked away.

Well, that was that, Jupe thought as he ordered the hot dogs, popcorn, and drinks. His chance to date a charming college girl was gone. Poof. There were no rewards for solving this case—not for anyone. Shoremont was going to lose, Pete was stuck with the Ark, Jupe was going back to Rocky Beach High . . .

Splash! Jupe heard the drinks spill, but all he saw was purple. Slowly he realized why—he had run right into Coach Duggan, who was wearing his purple Shoremont jacket and cap. Coach Duggan was now also wearing the cola Jupe had been carrying.

"I'm terribly sorry, Coach Duggan," Jupe started to say.

The coach's blue eyes didn't blink. "Don't worry about it, Jupiter," he said. "Cola settles the stomach. In fact, I ought to get some for the guys in my locker room. They'll need all the help they can get. You know, a few of them haven't played more than sixty seconds this season, but they're ready to do their best."

"Well, good luck, Coach," Jupe said.

The coach nodded. "You know, Jupe, I wanted to thank you personally for what you've done for me. I'm going into a play-off game minus some of my best players. We don't stand a snowball's chance of winning. But you know what? I feel good about it. I was innocent in Boston, and now I think everyone knows that I'm innocent here. I owe it to you—you've helped clear up both my reputation and this game."

"Well, it was nothing, really," Jupe said modestly.

Coach Duggan started to walk away, but then he turned back to say just one more thing.

"But you know what's going to be harder than replacing those players, Jupiter?"

Jupe shook his head.

"Finding an MVP like you!"

Jupe looked confused. "Most Valuable Player?"

"Most Valuable Parrot. You were the best!"